"I ne...
J...
I know it is."

"Are you su—" Bet blinked as another thought intruded. "Do you really need me, Jake?"

His lips curled into a soft smile. "I'm going to have a hard time having babies without you, Slugger. And now that I've met you, somehow I can't imagine having them with anyone else."

"I . . . I'm afraid," she whispered.

"So am I." Her expression of surprise drew a chuckle from him. "I want you to be happy, Bet. This may not be our great romance, but it can grow into something strong and lasting. I want that."

"So do I. More than anything."

"Then marry me, Slugger. I need you."

Delaney Devers *is a self-avowed daydreamer, since "gorgeous hunks never say the wrong thing when it's your dream." Embroidering on her daydreams ultimately led her to writing, which she considers both "hard work and pure pleasure." An Air Force wife, Delaney has led an extremely peripatetic life. She currently resides, writes, and daydreams in Louisiana.*

Dear Reader:

Exactly one year ago, at a time when romance readers were asking for "something different," we took a bold step in romance publishing by launching an innovative new series of books about married love: TO HAVE AND TO HOLD.

Since then, TO HAVE AND TO HOLD has developed a faithful following of enthusiastic readers. We're still delighted to receive your letters — which come from teenagers, grandmothers, and women of every age in between, both married and single. All of you have one quality in common — you believe that love and romance exist beyond the "happily ever after" endings of more conventional stories.

In the months to come, we will continue to offer romance reading of the highest caliber in TO HAVE AND TO HOLD. Keep an eye out for two books by our very popular Jeanne Grant — *Cupid's Confederates* in November and *Conquer the Memories* in December. And, as we've always done in TO HAVE AND TO HOLD, we've lined up some terrific new writers. In October we're bringing you *Deeper Than Desire* by newcomer Jacqueline Topaz, as well as a truly special, incredibly heartwarming romance, *The Heart Victorious* by Delaney Devers. In December we follow with a unique and witty story, *Tyler's Folly* by Joan Darling. We're especially proud to introduce these wonderfully talented writers to you — and pleased to publish more stories by the ever-welcome Charlotte Hines, Lee Williams, Katherine Granger, and Jennifer Rose.

At TO HAVE AND TO HOLD we have a lot to celebrate! But most of all, we want to thank all of you for your enthusiasm and support, which have made TO HAVE AND TO HOLD an ongoing success.

Warmest wishes,

Ellen Edwards

Ellen Edwards, Senior Editor
TO HAVE AND TO HOLD
The Berkley Publishing Group
200 Madison Avenue
New York, N.Y. 10016

THE HEART VICTORIOUS

DELANEY DEVERS

A
SECOND CHANCE AT LOVE
BOOK

THE HEART VICTORIOUS

First edition published October 1984

First printing

Printed in the United States of America

To Have and to Hold books are published by
The Berkley Publishing Group
200 Madison Avenue, New York, NY 10016

To My Husband, Frank
   for Love
   for Inspiration
   for Always Believing
   for patience, Patience, PATIENCE!

THE HEART
VICTORIOUS

STOLEN DREAMS

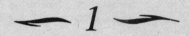

"Aw, c'mon, Bet. You can get a sitter for Bonnie just one night. Geez, it's gruesome the way you sit at home. C'mon, have some fun," Carrie wheedled.

"Tellers' night out does sound good, but I really can't." Bet Valentine smiled at her fellow bank teller, Carrie Brewster, and surreptitiously checked her digital watch. "And it isn't gruesome to stay with Bonnie. She's sitting up now and beginning to notice everything."

"Yeah, she's a doll, but..." Carrie flicked at her impossibly red hair with long violet nails and shifted her weight from one hip to the other. "Gee, Bet," she said softly, "John's been dead nearly a year now. You weren't buried with him, y'know. I'm awful worried about you."

"Thanks, Carrie. You don't know how much it's meant to me to have you for a friend. You've helped me through some rough times."

"Aw"— Carrie popped her gum and snapped a playful jab at Bet's arm—"what're friends for?"

Behind them, Mr. James, the bank manager, locked the door and came down the walk toward the parking lot, striding past the small prickly hedges at his usual brisk pace. "Good night, ladies. Or should I be calling you *persons* these days?"

"G'night, Mr. James," Carrie called out. "You can call me a person, but I think Bet still likes being called a lady. So don't you go forgetting to open doors for her."

"I won't," he laughed back over his shoulder. "And don't you go forgetting you like to open your own."

"Gee, ain't he a nice fella," Carrie said with a sigh. "If he was twenty years younger and single, I sure could go for him. Well, I know you're running late to pick up Bonnie, so I'll just mosey along, like those cowboys used to say. Sure wish you'd come tonight. We're gonna paint the town purple."

Bet laughed. "I thought that was red."

"Shooey, honey! Red's old hat!" Carrie's violet-colored lips slid into a wide grin, and with an exaggerated swing to her slender hips, she sauntered toward her car.

Bet scrambled through her oversize purse, pushing aside a Pampers, a teething ring, and a bottle half full of clabbered milk. Tonight, she promised herself, she would remember to take it out. Sweat dewed her forehead, and she raised her eyes to the glaring white sun. It was one of those southern spring days that looked and felt more like midsummer, with baking heat and stifling humidity beneath a pale, bleached sky.

She slid in behind the steering wheel of her sensible Sentra and put on her safety belt, double-checking the catch. Her lax hands curled lightly around the wheel, and she sat still for a moment, fighting down a surge of grief. If it weren't for Bonnie, she would just as soon be with John in his grave. He had done everything right. Everything! But it hadn't helped when that gravel truck crushed...

Bet knew it didn't do her any good to go over and over it. It just gave her dreams that woke her screaming in the night and upset Bonnie. John's baby, and he never even saw her. But he had wanted her desperately. He would have been such a good father, Bet thought with a sad smile, remembering the day she'd told him she was expecting. Nothing would do but that they go shopping right then. A bassinet, a crib, a chest of drawers, a playpen—he'd wanted to get it all. They'd made so many plans in that month before he died.

"It doesn't do any good to think about it, Bet Valentine," she told herself sternly. It doesn't do any good: It had been her litany for nearly a year.

She started the car and backed out of the bank lot, entering the stream of traffic while mentally ticking off the things she needed to do. Stop at the grocery store for Bonnie's formula and some kind of fodder for herself— she thought of food as little else these days. Tomorrow— another Saturday to trudge through—she would have to finish the manuscript she was typing for a local writer. Five hundred dollars. The work was worth every penny . . . and spent on the pediatrician and the nursery before it was made. Next month the car insurance was due. Bet rubbed at the ache between her eyes. Maybe she'd be able to scare up another manuscript. Otherwise she didn't know where the money would come from.

Lord, she hated it! It wasn't only the loneliness, although that was bad enough—sometimes she found herself dawdling at Mr. James's desk, just to hear the sound of a man's voice. It was pinching pennies and the constant worry about not having enough if Bonnie got sick. It was the gut-wrenching fear that *she* might get sick, and then what would happen to her daughter? It was seeing Bonnie mornings and evenings and weekends, while someone else watched her during the day. That was the worst: knowing that a stranger would lead Bonnie through her first steps and hear her first words.

She and John had planned it so differently. Neither had known a stable home life. After being abandoned by her mother when she was five, Bet had been raised in a succession of foster homes. Her single sustaining dream had been to have an old-fashioned family. No career for her. Her husband and her children and her home would be her career.

For John it had been different. He'd had a father and a mother and a house, which failed to classify as a home. His father was a pale shadow of a man who faded into insignificance beside John's mother. Nancy Valentine was a rabid women's libber whose proudest moment had been burning her bra in a sixties demonstration. She was a lawyer, and a good one, with no use for a woman who didn't want to claw her way to the top in a worthwhile career. And in Nancy's book, homemaking definitely didn't qualify. As a child, John had come home to an empty house every day. There was no one to bake cookies or take him to Scout meetings or Little League practice, although his mother did take him to consciousness-raising sessions at the tender age of eleven. He'd sworn that his children would be raised differently. They would know they were loved and wanted for themselves, not as symbols of the perfect woman who managed to combine home, family, and career.

Bet's and John's dreams meshed into one flawless whole. They wanted a large family sprawling through an old farmhouse. They wanted chickens and ducks and dogs. They wanted sneakers in the living room and skates on the stairs. They wanted the bedlam of getting the kids off to school in the morning and the peace of walking down the hall late at night, tucking their beloved monsters into bed and listening to their prayers. Their idea of heaven was taffy on the walls, chewing gum stuck to their shoes, and fingerprints on the refrigerator.

Then John was dead, and with him went the dream.

Bet swiped the tears from her cheeks and pulled into the parking lot of the nursery. Her dragging spirits lifted as she thought of Bonnie, waiting, all soft and sweet and rosy. Eagerness tripped through her, and she hopped from the car and ran to the door.

"I've come for Bonnie," she sang to the thin stick of a woman behind the counter. "Can I go back to get her?"

"No, Mrs. Valentine. You know it upsets the other children to see a parent come in. I'll bring Bonnie to you. Just have a seat and wait."

Bet perched on the edge of a vinyl chair with a torn flap spilling out stuffing. The door into the children's area swung open, and she heard a high-pitched scream. Bonnie! She'd know her daughter's cry anywhere! She pushed the door open and marched in, weaving around the cribs until she found her infant.

Three-month-old Bonnie flailed her chubby limbs and screamed her heart out. Her face was blotchy red. Vomit was crusted down her chin and on her cotton gown. Pools of mustardy excrement poured out of her diaper and streaked her pumping legs.

"Mrs. Valentine!" the nursery woman said huffily. "I asked you to wait!"

Bet peeled her fingers away from the crib and fought to catch her breath. "I can see why! This didn't just happen," she blazed. "Bonnie's been lying here like this for a long time. Give me that diaper!" She snatched it from the woman's hand and proceeded to clean Bonnie with a shaking hand. "What kind of people are you? Listening to a baby cry! Doing nothing! Letting it lie in its own vomit!" She lifted her freshly diapered daughter, cradling her in one arm while she jerked up the diaper bag. "You won't be seeing Bonnie here again!"

Bonnie went to sleep in her car seat, little sobbing breaths fluttering her tiny lips, and Bet fought back tears until she drove into the parking space in front of her town-house apartment. She sat there, staring at her door with dull, shimmering eyes. She would have to move to a cheaper place. There was nothing to be done for it. She couldn't settle for second best for Bonnie, and the best nurseries cost a fortune. Guilt was an aching weight in her breast, and she rested her head on the steering wheel and gave way to racking sobs that woke Bonnie, who began to squall along with her.

Something thumped against the car window, and Bet raised her head, sniffed mightily, and rolled down the window.

"Bet dear, whatever is wrong with you?" her neighbor,

Mrs. March, asked in her thick, old-time Southern drawl.

"Everything!" she answered dramatically.

"Oh, I doubt that." Mrs. March smiled. "Is there anything I can do?"

"I could use someone to talk to. Would you open the door while I get Bonnie?"

While Bet bathed her daughter and readied her for bed, soothed somewhat by Bonnie's gleeful cooing and chuckling, Mrs. March ran next door for sassafras to brew tea, her favorite remedy for "the blues, the blahs, and anything else that ails you."

A short time later, with Bonnie upstairs sleeping, Bet and Mrs. March drank their tea in the living room. "I'm a failure, Mrs. March." Bet raked her hand through the short, crisp waves of her bronze-colored hair. "I tried so hard to find a good nursery for Bonnie. The workers all seemed so pleasant, and it was a place I could afford. But look what happened!"

She leaned her head back against the rose velvet couch. "I'm a freak. I hate working. I just want to stay home and raise my daughter. I don't want to compete on a man's level in a man's world." She sighed and stared up at the ceiling. "If this were a hundred years ago, I'd answer an ad for a mail-order bride."

"Oh, Bet, you can't mean that."

"I do, Mrs. March. I really do."

"My dear, a loveless union?"

Bet raised her head to look at her neighbor. Hester March was a little cricket of a woman with a prim white bun. She combined warm motherliness with an offbeat, unpredictable sense of humor. "I had enough love with John to last me a lifetime. I don't need that again. If I found a man I could respect, who would love Bonnie as his own, and would want the same things from life that I do, I'd marry him in a minute."

"Love might grow from that."

"No, I won't ever love like that again. It hurts too

much to lose it." Bet sat up, drained her tea, and gave Mrs. March a smile tinged with sadness. "I don't know whether it's the sympathetic ear or your sassafras tea, but I do feel better."

"Maybe it's a little of both. I wish I weren't leaving for my sister's tomorrow. What will you do about work Monday if you can't find a nursery before then?"

"I don't know, but that isn't for you to worry about. You just have a good time."

"Oh, that I will." Hester March laughed. "Esther has three boys and seven grandchildren. We always have one of those 'Ya'll come' get-togethers with family and friends and friends of friends. Jake—that's her oldest boy—he raises the best beef..." Her voice trailed away, and a speculative gleam began to twinkle in the puckish blue eyes behind her wire-rimmed glasses. "Oh, yes, I do believe I will enjoy this visit," she murmured before taking a demure sip of her tea.

The lawn stretching from the stately old house to the weed-choked ditch beside the gravel road, which was slightly hazy with dust from the latest arrival, was swarming with people. Children played tag and blindman's buff. Women gossiped around picnic tables laden with salads, vegetables, and desserts. Men hunkered down in groups to discuss the hot weather and the prices of beef and hay.

Jake Calloway stood on the outer rim of the group, alone. He propped one scuffed cowboy boot on a low stump, resting his forearm on his thigh. As he pushed his battered Stetson farther back on his thick black hair, his gaze moved slowly from one familiar face to the other. Aunts, uncles, cousins, neighbors—he knew them all, had known them all his life. Yet he had a curious reluctance to join them. The reluctance wasn't new to him. It was years old and growing worse.

It was the memories, he thought, as he picked out couples in the milling throng. The memories were always worse on this kind of day when it seemed everyone was half of a matched pair. His thoughts drifted along the twists and turns of the dusty gravel road to the little country church with its steeple and bell . . . and the tiny graveyard with its white picket fence.

His Tricia was there. For six years he had been alone, his gregarious nature slowly succumbing to the blighting shadow of his loneliness. It wasn't good for a man to be alone. Everyone told him that, and he knew it was true. Even Tricia . . .

How could a memory be so painful after so long? Didn't the ache ever go away? He could hear and see and feel it as though it were happening now. Tricia lying in the hospital bed, his sun-browned hand smoothing the sweaty strings of dark hair from her forehead. He could feel the febrile strength of her feverish hands clutching at his arm. He could hear her throaty whisper. *"Jake, promise me you'll marry again. Don't say no! Listen to me. It isn't good for a man to be alone. I want you to be happy. I want you to love and be loved. Promise me you'll marry again, without guilt, without regret. Don't you see? That will be your greatest tribute to what we've shared. Promise me, Jake."*

He had promised. He had lied. How could he marry again when what he had shared with Tricia had been perfection beyond his wildest dreams? How could he marry again when he'd given Tricia all the love he had to give? It was hard, being alone. Harder than he ever would have imagined. Sometimes he wished . . .

"Uncle Jake! Uncle Jake!"

He stirred from his waking dream and stared down at the miniature version of himself that came racing across the yard. He lowered his foot and braced himself. The heavy weight of sadness lifted and vanished. His wide mouth curved into a smile of welcome, and he raised his arms. His nephew, Archie, launched into a leap from a yard away, scrambled across Jake's shoulders, and snatched his hat from his head.

"Giddyup, Uncle Jake!"

Jake hooked his hands over Archie's battered tennis shoes and grinned at his nephew. "Where do you want to go?"

"Aunt Hester's looking for you. She's sitting at the picnic table with Grandma."

Jake's long stride carried them into the crowd. "What did she want me for?"

"Dunno. Something about matches. Can't you go faster?" Archie pumped up and down on his shoulders as Jake approached the tables.

"It's Jake, and you know how he—" His mother's soft voice broke off. "Oh, here's Jake now."

"Did I hear someone taking my name in vain? Ouch!" He arched his black eyebrows up at Archie, who had just yanked his hair.

"Giddyup, Uncle Jake!"

"I'm gonna *giddy* your *up* if you yank me bald, Archie Calloway! You want to have half the girls in this parish crying because I lost my looks?"

"Girls! Yuk!"

Jake eased his nephew from the perch of his broad shoulders and chuckled. "Come tell me that in a few years' time. Now, scat, cat! I've got to flirt with Aunt Hester." He gave his nephew a playful swat on the behind to send him on his way. Instead of turning to his aunt, Jake stood watching the boy scamper across the lawn and jump onto the old tire swinging from a pine, and he knew a moment of intense yearning.

When he turned away, he found his aunt watching him with bright-eyed interest. Of everyone he knew, Aunt Hester best understood how he felt, and that understanding had forged a strong bond between them. He grinned broadly.

"Hi, beautiful! I sure wish we weren't related. I'd pick you up and carry you off to my castle."

"Drafty old things. Never did like them," she retorted, peering over the gold rims of her glasses with sparkling, puckish blue eyes. "I see you haven't changed since the last time I saw you. Still long, lean, lanky, and gorgeous."

Jake hooted with laughter. "And you wonder why I want to carry you off." Still chuckling, he sank to the ground to sit Indian-fashion. "Archie said you wanted to see me. Something about matches." The conspiratorial, self-satisfied look Aunt Hester flashed at his mother stopped Jake in mid-thought. Matches? *Matchmaking!* Damn! Caution leaped into him like a panther a moment after crouching on a branch, waiting with a silent deadly flick of its tail.

Hester leaned forward, her hands pressed together prayerfully. "Jake, are you still seeing that girl—"

"No."

"Oh, goo—I mean . . ." She looked flustered for a moment. "No, I do mean good. She wasn't the girl for you."

"Ahh." Jake grinned, torn between frustration and amusement. "But you know one who is?"

"Oh, yes!" She clasped her hands beneath her chin and beamed. "Perfect!"

Jake felt his smile become a little strained. "Would it do any good to tell you I don't want to hear about her?"

"None whatsoever!"

In all these years, his Aunt Hester was the only one who hadn't set her hand to matchmaking. That she suddenly would now piqued his curiosity, a curiosity he dared not reveal. Aunt Hester had the tenacity of a bulldog when she thought she was right, and she was obviously enthused about something.

"Tell me about this paragon of perfection," Jake groaned.

"First you tell me why you haven't remarried."

His whole posture changed, withdrawing, closing in, yet still preparing him to defend himself. Glancing down at the muscles rippling from his rolled-up plaid sleeves, down his arms, and across his clenching fists, he growled, "You know why."

"I must know if you've changed your mind."

"No. I can't marry a woman who expects a love I can't give her."

"My dear boy, I had three husbands, and I loved them all to distraction. Each held a separate—"

"Aunt Hester, we've discussed this before. I don't want to hear it again."

"So we have," she said, obviously undaunted by the low vibrato of anger in his voice. "I heard words very like yours a few days ago from a young widow. My neighbor, Bet Valentine." She proceeded to tell him what she knew of Bet's history, her marriage, and her present circumstances, ending with their last conversation. "So you see, she's a bride made to order for you. Neither of you wants love, but you both want children and the kind of home that sounds quite outdated in this modern world. This is an opportunity that will be a long time coming, if it ever does again. Do think about it, Jake."

At that moment Archie came running up and threw himself into Jake's lap, wrapping his thin arms around his uncle's neck. "Gimme a ride, Uncle Jake. Gimme a ride!"

Jake hugged his nephew and raked tendrils of coal-black hair off the child's face. Children? Yes, he wanted children of his own. His nephews and nieces—no matter that they were in and out of his house as much as their own—could not appease his growing hunger. The hunger had grown so strong, he had even given serious thought to having a baby by a surrogate mother. But he couldn't do it. A child needed a mother and a stable home.

He met his aunt's watchful eyes. Was this the answer? A marriage comprised of companionship, respect, and the satisfaction of mutual needs? A woman who didn't expect love from him, and who wouldn't be willing to give it? Marriages had succeeded with far less. His gaze dropped to the child on his lap. Hunger fed on hope.

"I don't need to think about it, Aunt Hester. I'll drive you to Shreveport next Saturday and meet this one and only opportunity."

Jake Calloway stood in the center of his Aunt Hester's sunny kitchen with his hands hanging loose at his sides. She tugged his black and white pin-striped shirt across the width of his shoulders and smoothed a wrinkle from his charcoal-gray slacks.

"I remember Mama doing this on my first date when I was fourteen, but even she thinks thirty-four is a little old for having one's fingernails and behind one's ears checked."

Hester swatted him on the rear. "I haven't checked your nails or behind your ears. Should I?"

"Lord," he groaned, "I'm giving her ideas!"

She skipped around him and stopped in front of him, her twinkling eyes taking on a roguish aspect as they climbed all the way upward from the mirror shine of his black leather shoes. A finger tapped her chin. "Now, what is it the girls say these days?" She thought a minute. "Oh, I know! You're a hunk, Jake Calloway!"

"Aunt Hester!" he shouted with laughter. "When are you going to start acting your age?"

"I am. It's all up here." She tapped her head with her forefinger. "Come on, let's go."

"Oh, no!" Jake said, perfectly willing to indulge her but not this far. "I will make my own introduction in my own way. All I need is you standing around looking like the cat that got the canary. Mrs. Valentine and I are not starry-eyed teenagers looking for our one and only love. We're sensible adults—"

"Sensible! Humph!"

He frowned. "Yes, sensible adults looking for a relationship built on mutual respect, and that is how I intend to approach her."

"But—"

"No *buts!* You stay!" He winked and started for the

front door. "I promise to tell you all about it."

"Wouldn't you like to know where she is?" Aunt Hester drawled with a touch of acid.

"I can't get her by ringing the front doorbell?"

"You could, but she's working in the backyard. Just go out through my gate and turn left. She's right next door." She slid the screen open. "And watch out for that concrete block laid up against the fence. I've tripped over it more times that I can tell."

Jake gave her a jaunty wave and closed the gate behind him. Somehow, in the few steps to the next gate, the jauntiness oozed out of him. He stood outside the six-foot privacy fence, a frown cleaving a crease between his brows.

He must have been crazy to think he could bring another woman into Tricia's house, into Tricia's bed, into his life. He closed his eyes and pictured his sprawling ranch-style house. He felt the emptiness and heard the hollow sounds of a man rattling around alone in the wide, deep rooms that had been planned with so much shared laughter and so many shared dreams. He thought of the bedrooms, three deep, marching in pairs down the hall. And he thought of those doors, shut against the silence in rooms planned for the children he and Tricia never had the chance to have. He felt the dull ache of loneliness, and his hand twitched and began to move against his will.

His fingers closed around the wrought-iron handle of the gate, and Jake stared at his hand. A callus curved around the pad of his thumb. Wiry black hair crawled in a thick matting down his arm and across the backs of his fingers. It was a large hand, and strong, but it was capable of drifting lightly over a woman's soft, perfumed flesh and speaking its own language of tenderness and gentle passion.

Jake's fingers clenched tight, as though his hand would force him to reach out for whatever awaited him beyond that gate. But his mind instructed him differently, urging his fingers to uncurl, to reject anything that might blur the bright image of Tricia. He shoved his hand into his pocket and began to turn away.

A baby's gurgling laughter stopped him in his tracks. He listened and heard a woman's voice. It was a soft voice, light and sweet and loving. A voice to warm a man and waken those dormant dreams of home and hearth cluttered with laughing children. Curiosity pumped at Jake's heels, and he looked over the top of the fence.

The tiny yard was so neat it looked manicured. Morning glories climbed strings stapled to the fence, and geraniums bloomed in a long row fronted by lush purple petunias. The baby, pink and plump, chewed her toes in a carrier atop a redwood table, and the woman knelt with her back to him, digging in a bed of vegetables with a trowel.

Her short-cropped hair was a deep bronze color, fiery red and gold where the sun stroked it with a bright hand. She wore white shorts and a blousy white terry-cloth tube top. Jake stared at the smooth honey-colored skin of her back and the slightly darker gold of her legs, and his fingers curled into his itching palms. She was slender, but the hips that sank back on her bare heels swelled enticingly from a tiny waist.

She stretched, arching her back, and Jake Calloway's breath shortened. She brushed the back of her hand across her forehead and dragged it over the crisp waves of her hair, and he swallowed hard. She extended her arms and dropped her head back, rolling it from side to side while her back moved in sinuous, sensuous curves. He licked suddenly dry lips, wondering how so simple a thing as arching and stretching could be so...so...erotic. The answering warmth from his inflamed mind licked into his belly, and she dropped her arms, leaned over the bed, and began digging.

The spell shattered. A flush of embarrassment invaded Jake's cheeks, and he cursed under his breath, ashamed of peeking over the fence like a voyeur. Frowning, he glanced away and saw the baby trying to roll over in the teetering carrier, which was perilously near the edge of the table.

He yanked at the gate, found it locked, opened his mouth to yell, moved, and stumbled over the concrete block. Stepping onto it, he vaulted over the fence and raced across the yard, snatching the baby into his arms. The infant gave him a toothless laugh, balled up her fist, and split his lip—which wasn't the end of Jake Calloway's problems.

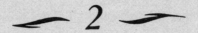

2

SOMETHING HARD THUNKED painfully into the middle of Jake's back while something nasty, wet, and cold snapped around his arm and an ear-splitting shriek clawed at his eardrums.

"Help! Police! Baby-snatcher!"

Jake cradled the infant, one large hand shielding her head, as he turned to explain himself. He opened his mouth, and a mop slapped across his face and wrapped around the back of his neck.

"Call the police! Somebody call the police! Baby-snatcher! Baby-snatcher!"

Jake shook his head and spit, caught a good look at the wild-eyed lunatic brandishing the mop, and began backing away. "Look, lady—"

"Pervert! Put my baby down! Now! Help! Help!"

Jake stepped on a petunia, trod on a geranium, and thumped up against the fence, the tightly wrapped petals of a morning glory tickling his ear while the mop swayed dangerously near his nose. "Okay, lady, okay. I'll give her to you. Just—"

"No. Put her on the grass and back off!"

Tawny eyes with the bright glitter of fury never left his face as Jake inched into a stoop, careful to do nothing to startle the woman. The gurgling baby began screaming the moment he laid her down. He quickly raised his hands, eased himself up, and began edging out of the flower bed, coming to a stop a few feet away.

"Lady, my na—"

She snarled and charged like a pole vaulter, aiming her mop at a most sensitive spot. Jake's eyes widened and hastily he side-stepped and caught the head of the mop. "Aunt Hester, I know you've got your eye glued to the knothole!" he bellowed. "Tell this woman who I am!"

Hester March's head popped over the fence.

Bet snatched the mop from his hand, darted a glance toward her neighbor, then pierced him with a narrow-eyed glare. "Do you know this man, Mrs. March?"

Hester gave her nephew her most innocent smile. "Can't say as I do, dear. He looks like a pervert to me."

"Aunt Hester!" Jake roared. "This is no time to be funny! Tell her who I am!"

Hester sighed loudly, twinkling eyes peeking over the rim of her glasses. "I do hate to admit it, Bet, but this...this um...this pervert is my nephew, Jake Calloway. Jake, I'd like you to meet Elizabeth Valentine. Her friends call her Bet. Maybe you can, too—eventually. Oh, and that baby you were trying to steal, that's Bonnie. Well, I think I'll leave you two young people to get acquainted. Oh, here comes Mr. Gerald." She raised her voice. "It's nice to know our neighbors will come when we need them, but you can put your gun away, Mr. Gerald. It was all a dreadful mistake. And there's that nice Mr. Fitzmorris with his baseball bat. Yoo-hoo, Mr. Fitzmorris. It was all a mistake."

"You sure, Mrs. March? Bet sounded mighty scared."

"Oh, yes. It was just my nephew going calling." She wagged her fingers at a fuming Jake and popped out of sight, then popped back up like a jack-in-the-box for a parting shot. "I must admit your approach has a certain flair."

Jake gnashed his teeth, promising himself he would find a way to get even, but a single look at Bet soothing her wailing daughter set all such thoughts to flight. She was a beauty when she wasn't snarling like an enraged tigress. Not a sleek, classic beauty like Tricia. Her eyes were too big and her nose too small for that. The dusting of freckles from cheek to cheek gave her small face an aura of innocence and vulnerability. He almost laughed aloud. There had been nothing either innocent or vulnerable in the way she charged him with that mop.

He rolled his shoulders to ease the ache in the middle of his back. She packed a mean wallop. A glint of admiration brightened his eyes. There she was, half his weight and a good foot shorter, but he had no doubt she would have successfully fought him off if he had been intent on baby-snatching.

A smile tugged at his lips. He knew all he needed to know about *Slugger* Valentine. She was one hell of a mother—and that was all he wanted. One week—two at the most—they could get the I do's behind them; then they could start filling those empty rooms.

Soothing her daughter, Bet rested her flushed cheek atop Bonnie's head, her trembling fingers touching a downy cheek, encompassing a small arm, rubbing the soft warmth of her daughter's back. She ached to wrap her up in a tight hug, but Bonnie had calmed down, and she didn't want to frighten her all over again.

Bet's heart thrummed against her eardrums while the terror, unlike anything she had ever experienced, slowly oozed away. In its place came irritation, scrabbling along her nerves with tiny mice feet. Her lips curved down at the corners, and a frown creased her brow as she stared at the cause of the commotion, deciding she didn't like big, dark men. How dare he stand there with that silly grin after he'd scared her half to death?

"Why did you come in here and pick up Bonnie?" she

asked, not attempting to conceal her rising anger.

"I was coming over to introduce myself. When I looked over the fence..." There was a curious pause, during which his liquid black eyes drifted across Bet's face, intense, seeking. The spots of color on her cheeks grew warmer. "Uh..." he said, looking away. "When I looked over the gate, she was trying to roll over. The carrier was too close to the edge of the table, and there wasn't time to do anything but jump the fence and try to get her before she fell."

Tawny eyes, tinged with a tigerish yellow, flicked toward the fence. "Quite a jump."

"I was a high jumper in high school, but that was a long time ago." A smile played around his lips. "Good thing I had that block to give me a boost."

"Good thing," she sniped. "And I would have sworn you were a quarterback," she added with a cattiness that amazed her. Why was she acting like this? He had saved Bonnie from a nasty fall, and it was all she could do to keep herself from leaping at him to scratch the glitter of amusement from those black eyes.

"Oh," he said casually through a breaking smile, "that, too."

"I suppose I owe you an apology," she said grudgingly.

Thick eyebrows climbed away from the sparkle in his eyes, and Bet's anger drained away so rapidly she was left weak-kneed, exhausted, and ashamed of herself. The icy pebbling of a cold sweat burst on her forehead, and she began to feel as if she were on a whirling carousel. She shook her head to clear the fuzziness from it. "I'm sorry for being so rude. I don't..." Her shaking hand swept across her forehead. "I don't know what...got into me. I do apologize and thank...thank you."

She could feel the blood draining from her cheeks. Her knees wobbled beneath her, and she felt his hand, warm and strong, around her arm.

"Hey, Slugger, are you all right?"

"No," she whispered, "I don't think I am." She breathed in gulping breaths, like a long-distance runner. "I feel . . . I feel . . ." She began to sag, and everything blurred and blackened.

Bet woke on her couch with her feet propped over the arm rest, a pillow beneath her hips, and a blanket covering her. Her first thought was a scintillating starburst of agony. Her arms were empty! She lurched into a sitting position, her wide, wild gaze racing around the room. Bonnie slept on her stomach in the playpen, her thumb tucked into her mouth. Bet went weak with relief.

She caught a glimpse of gray slacks around the corner of the kitchen door, and everything returned in a breath-taking rush. Hearing a thump. Whirling around to see a strange man trying to make away with her daughter. That first paralyzing terror . . .

What if he had been taking Bonnie and she had been frozen, unable to move from that spot? Dear God, what if someone *had* taken Bonnie? Her vivid imagination conjured a quiet house . . . an empty crib . . . silent rattles . . .

The trembling began deep in the pit of her stomach, spreading outward in concentric circles until she shook from head to toe. Her teeth chattered audibly, and an icy sweat popped from every pore.

At that moment Jake came in, carrying a tray with two steaming cups. He took one look at her, set the tray on the coffee table, and knelt on the floor beside her. Helping her sit up, he tugged the blanket around her and began chafing her hands. "It hit you, didn't it? I really could have been a baby-snatcher."

"Y-y-yes," she hissed through chattering teeth. "I d-don't th-th-think I've ever b-b-been so s-s-scared in my life."

"You couldn't prove it by me," he laughed softly. "I was the one being beaten with the mop."

"I d-d-don't know what I w-w-would do if I l-lost

Bonnie." Her eyes brimmed with crystalline tears that began spilling over her dusky lashes and flooding her cheeks.

"Here, now." Jake sat on the couch, lifting her onto his lap, blanket and all. "There, cry it all out. You'll feel better."

And Bet Valentine buried her face in the board-hard chest of a perfect stranger and sobbed until she nearly made herself sick. What was worse, it felt good. Little things kept creeping around the edge of her tears to spread blossoms of warmth. The strength of his long brown arms wrapping her in heavenly security. The gentleness of the big hand rubbing up and down her back. The smell of a man unmarred by spicy cologne. The tickle of wiry black hair curling out of the V of his shirt to tantalize her forehead. The slow, easy rise and fall of his chest. It had been so long, and it felt so good.

Her sobbing died down to hiccuping breaths, and she found the most godawful red, black, and yellow plaid handkerchief being pressed into her hand. Bet arched a bleary eye up at Jake's beard-shadowed chin.

"Blow." He grinned. "You look worse than my nephew Archie when he's got a cold."

She eyed the handkerchief with patent disbelief, gingerly took it between two fingers, and felt the rippling of laughter surging through his chest before it sounded, warm and deep.

"I have a drawer full of them," he explained. "Birthday and Christmas presents from Archie. He doesn't think his Uncle Jake should use boring white handkerchiefs."

Bet smiled and blew into it.

"Feel better?" he asked gently.

Bet lay her head back on his arm. "Much better."

Their eyes met and locked, liquid black and shining tawny brown. Tension zinged in the air, and Bet's heart did a little skipping beat before it took off like a racehorse leaving the gate. Some indefinable emotion flickered in the depths of his eyes, and her lips parted for a fluttering breath. His mouth moved closer...closer... he blurred, and her lashes began drifting across her shining eyes. His breath was warm on her lips and his heart pounded against her arm and his mouth touched hers, gently, oh, so gently—and the doorbell rang.

They sprang apart, staring at each other like guilty children caught red-handed. Bet's face flamed, and a flush ruddied Jake's dark skin. "Who...who do you think it could be?" she whispered. Immediately she could have kicked herself.

His puzzled look turned to one of dawning realization. A smile spread across his face, cleaving deep creases in his cheeks. "I'd bet my last nickel it's the police."

"Oh, no!" Bet popped off of his lap and ran to the door, trailing the blanket.

"Good morning, ma'am. We had a call that—"

"Oh, I'm so sorry!" Bet exclaimed breathlessly. "It was all a mistake. I should have called. You see, this man saw my baby falling and caught her and I thought...I thought he was trying to steal her."

"You're sure everything is all right?"

"Oh, yes, officer! It was a misunderstanding."

Bet shut the door and returned to the living room. Her eyes skittered away from any contact with Jake's. "It was the police," she said, suddenly very busy folding the blanket into neat quarters.

"I heard. Here, have your coffee."

She put the blanket aside, took a cup from the tray, eyed the couch, and moved away to the safety of an armchair. Tucking her bare feet beneath her, she took a sip of the muddy-looking liquid. Lukewarm. Ugh.

His dark eyes watched her intently, and Bet's hand trembled around the cup. It was ridiculous, she assured herself, but it didn't help. She still felt as shy as a gawky girl.

"I'm...I'm fortunate that my neighbors were so willing to help." She ended on a squeak and blushed hotly.

"Very," he said quietly, adding nothing more, which increased her discomfort.

She wriggled around in the chair, took another sip of the cold coffee, and cast about desperately for some topic that might ease the clumsy silence. "You—you said you were coming over to introduce yourself. Why?"

Bet watched his face and saw a flicker of indecision that hardened into a resolve that seemed to give him some amusement. A twinkle starred his black eyes, and his smile grew wide once again.

"I was coming to look you over."

"Look me over?" Bet gasped. "Why?"

"Will you marry me, Bet Valentine?"

Her jaw sagged, and her dusky lashes climbed to her eyebrows. "You may not be a pervert, but you are, beyond all doubt, crazy!"

"Hereditary," Jake drawled with a wink. "Comes from Aunt Hester's side of the family." The twinkle of amusement faded from his dark eyes. Slowly his heavy eyebrows eased together, pinching a single crease above the bridge of his nose. "I'm a widower, Bet," he said quietly.

The cutting edge of hostility in her glittering stare gave way to confusion and softened with sympathy. "I'm sorry. I know..." She toyed with the blurring rim of her cup. "You see, I lost my husband recently."

"Aunt Hester told me. She thinks you and I would make the perfect couple, and now that I've met you, so do I."

Empathy vanished on a cresting peak of revulsion. Bet recoiled in her chair, giving him a hard, wary look. "You don't know me, Mr. Calloway."

"I know more about you than you think." Her brown eyes questioned, and Jake grinned. "Our guardian angel, Aunt Hester."

"I'm sure she meant well, but—"

"But she's a nosy interfering busybody?" He relaxed against the couch, long lashes veiling his eyes.

Bet tried not to notice the way his shirt pulled across the width of his shoulders or the way his lips promised to smile or the lazy way the muscled length of his arm was draped across the back of the couch or the way his long dark fingers spread across the dusky rose velvet. Her reluctant gaze slid back along his arm to the swell of his shoulder, touched the lean square of his jaw, and moved to his lips. Her tongue peeped out. Had she really kissed those...

"We're better matched than you know," he said suddenly. "Will you let me start at the beginning?"

Her wandering thoughts snapped like a rubber band, and she stiffened against the sting of conscience. Tilting her freckled nose, she leveled a hostile stare. "This is better entertainment than Saturday afternoon baseball. Go ahead."

"My wife and I met while we were students at LSU. We were married while I was in graduate school. Three years later we returned to my home, built our own house, and settled down to what we thought would be a long and happy life. A year later we learned she was pregnant and..." He cleared the roughness from his throat and stared down at the clenched fist pressing into his thigh. "God, she was happy," he grated out, looking away. A deep breath swelled his chest and sighed out unsteadily. "One day she was near the pond on our place, alone. She was bitten by a diamondback rattler."

His lashes snapped down over his eyes, and Bet watched him struggle, his throat working. "Dammit!" The word burst from him like a bullet. "Nobody dies of that now!"

It was a cry of grief and rage and impotence, a cry that touched Bet deeply. Hadn't she felt all those things after John's death? She stared into the dregs in her cup, pain, anger, and helplessness surging as fresh as they had been on the day a policeman came to her door to say, "Mrs. Valentine, there has been an accident..."

"I'm sorry," Jake murmured, "I didn't mean to..."

"Don't be." Bet blinked back tears. "I'm sure many people have told you, as they've told me, that they know how you must feel. They had no idea, but I do. I loved my husband. When I lost him, there was an—an emptiness that even Bonnie hasn't been able to fill. It was as if . . . as if my life came to a stop on the day he died."

"But it didn't, Bet, and neither did mine. No matter how much we sometimes wish it had. We're young and healthy and alive. We have years before us. Years that we can waste, regretting what might have been, or years we could spend together, building a life than gives us satisfaction."

Bet frowned into his compelling stare. "You . . . you're serious!" she accused.

"Yes. I believe you and I can give each other what we most want. I need children, Bet. I want them raised in a stable home as I was raised, with both a father and a mother. And I want you to be that mother."

"But . . . but people don't marry like this!"

"Why not?"

"Because . . . because we don't know anything about each other!"

A smile quirked his lips. "I knew you were perfect the minute you charged me with that mop."

Bet's face flamed. "That is hardly a testimonial for motherhood!"

"I disagree." He gave her an infuriating grin. "As for me, just ask Aunt Hester. She'll tell you I'm gorgeous, modest, and the best catch of any year. If you're more practical than she is, I raise Brahmans, Herefords, horses, and hay with my father and two brothers. We have several thousand acres with some productive oil and gas wells. So you needn't worry that I can't support you and Bonnie and as many more children as you want. I have a ranch-style house with six bedrooms and a country kitchen, located on the west end of the Calloway Huddle. That's what we call a mile-long stretch of gravel road where my parents, my brothers, and I all have our houses."

Without realizing it, Jake had appealed to Bet's most deep-seated need. She leaned forward, her coffee cup clutched in both hands. There was an eagerness in her posture and a kind of hunger in her eyes. "Tell me about your family," she whispered.

He stared at her for a moment, then gave her a slow

smile. "I'll do better than that, but remember, you asked for it!" He dug his wallet out of his back pocket, held it up, and let it fall open. Plastic pockets filled with pictures tumbled to the floor in accordion pleats. "Come over here." Jake patted the couch, and Bet hurried to join him.

She leaned against his arm, entranced by a small dark-haired niece blowing out the candles on a birthday cake, a nephew grinning from the saddle of a Shetland pony, another decked out in a football uniform several sizes too large. There was a picture of Jake holding a baby and staring in dismay at the wet stain spread across his blue denim workshirt. There was another picture of Jake, this time with a small replica of himself riding on his shoulders.

"That's Archie," he told her. "Archie of the plaid handkerchief."

Bet flicked him a bright-eyed glance and turned back to the photographs. There were school pictures and studio pictures and candid snapshots. Smiling faces, secure and happy, a record of picnics and family reunions and softball games in grassy fields. They brought an ache to Bet's throat.

"These are my parents."

Bet stared at the tall, leathery skinned, white-haired man with a cowboy boot braced on a bench and an elbow propped on his thigh who smiled down at a tiny cricket of a woman who . . .

"She looks like Mrs. March!" Bet said in surprise.

"Twins."

"Oh," she breathed, her finger trembling as she reached out to touch the picture. "You don't know how lucky you are, Jake."

He liked the sound of his name on her lips. It was softer somehow. Jake stared at the curve of her cheek and saw the sheen of a tear glistening through the crescent of her lashes. He remembered what Aunt Hester had told him of Bet's childhood, and he tried to imagine what it would have been like to have no one, to be batted about from stranger to stranger. It was a chilling prospect, and he gave thanks for the sometimes irritating but always loving family he had taken for granted. He smiled a secret smile and dangled the bait of a family portrait that included everyone from Great-grandma Calloway to the youngest toddler.

"Say yes, Bet, and you marry them, too."

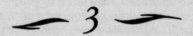

3

BET HOOKED THE heels of her sling-back pumps over the
rung of the tall stool. Staring at an antiseptic white wall,
she began counting ten-dollar bills on a gold-speckled
Formica surface. The mellow strains of mood music softened the crisp, no-nonsense modernity of the bank's in-
terior. The only jarring note—and one Bet welcomed—
was the sultry, musky scent of Carrie's perfume as she
clicked by on pencil-thin heels to take her station at the
counter facing the chrome and glass lobby.

Ten, twenty, thirty... laughing black eyes... forty,
fifty... uncompromising jaw... sixty... Will you marry
me, Bet Valentine... seventy... Say yes, and you marry
them, too...

Bet gave up the effort, laid the money aside, and
propped her chin on her hands. She was tempted. Oh,
was she tempted! It had been a week since she sat in her
living room listening to Jake's outrageous proposal.
Somehow, as one day melted into the next in his virile,

laughing presence, it seemed less and less outrageous, in spite of Mrs. March's vocal disapproval of Jake's strange method of courting. Bet didn't find it strange at all. She had never laughed so much nor felt so carefree nor felt so safe as she did when Jake's dark, liquid eyes touched her with a smile. And Bonnie adored him, forsaking even her mother when he was around to toss her into the air or cradle her on his broad shoulder.

Yes, Jake Calloway had made his mark on her life . . .

On Sunday they went to the amusement park. While Mrs. March watched over Bonnie in her stroller, Jake and Bet laughed their way from ride to ride until she was flushed and breathless. They sat on a bench in the shade of an umbrella, devouring hot dogs dripping with mustard and relish. He told her about the Calloway Fourth of July celebrations. A beef roasting on a spit for the adults; a bonfire for the grandchildren to roast wieners and marshmallows; a long lazy afternoon whiled away, with children cooling off under the lawn sprinklers and the adults playing softball after short naps under the pines.

Bet forgot to eat her hot dog while she drank in his every word, hungry eyes watching the firm lips that spilled magic into her imagination. She could see the women gathered around the wreckage of the picnic tables, the men dozing in the shade, and Bonnie, a toddler, squealing and tripping through the cool shower from the sprinklers. It was a vision of heaven. Jake's snapping fingers brought her back to the present. "Eat," he commanded with a grin before he left, returning minutes later with a candied apple. Before he was done teaching Bonnie how to lick it, they all stuck to everything they touched.

On Monday, after work, they took burgers, fries, and shakes to Clyde Fant Parkway on the rusty Red River. There Jake told her about Calloway Halloweens. Bet absorbed every word with parted lips and hands squeezed into eager fists. She could almost see his father with his battered straw hat, driving the tractor pulling the huge wagon strewn with hay along the gravel roads between far-flung neighbors, the children spilling off to trick or treat while their parents lay in the hay beneath the harvest moon.

Tuesday night Jake bought steaks to cook out in Bet's backyard—insisting she hide that dangerous weapon, her mop, before he would set foot through the gate. While Aunt Hester watched over Bonnie, lying on a quilt outside, Bet put on potatoes to steam, and Jake mixed up his special, secret sauce to baste the meat. The buttery-bright kitchen was hardly more than a niche, and Bet backed into Jake, her buttocks pressing against the backs of his thighs.

He skewed a look over his shoulder, his black eyes sparkling with laughter. "None of that now, woman. You're disturbing an artist at work."

Bet arched away, her face burning, less from his teasing then from the tingling that quivered in the pit of her stomach. She moved down the counter, fidgeting fingers snapping crisp lettuce into a bowl. Her lips pursed in thought; a frown tugged at her eyebrows. She drew a mental picture of her husband, John, seeing his ever sensitive features, the haunting loneliness in the depths of his pale eyes, a loneliness even she had not been able to erase. There had been very little laughter with John. Only a placid serenity, the haven of security she needed so much after the constant uprootings of her childhood.

But into those thoughts intruded the image of Jake Calloway. Firm, bold, dark, he was a man sure of himself and his place in the world. Yet, behind the laughter, Bet sensed a gnawing loneliness and knew that, like John, he would not find her enough to fill the empty space in his heart. The idea was curiously disturbing. While one part of her rejected the pain of loving again, another part capriciously insisted that she wanted to be the very center of someone's world. And being the center of Bonnie's was not enough. It had to be a man—a man who found her the source of his happiness, the fulfillment of his life. She felt the oh, so familiar despondency press upon her spirits. How could she expect that of a man when her own mother had rejected her?

"Slugger?"

Jake's voice was soft and concerned, as were the liquid eyes that held her upturned gaze. His finger traced the downward curve of her lip with a feathery touch. "Have I said something to hurt you?"

"No." She avoided his hand and buried her chin in her neck, blinking back the sting of tears.

He turned her gently, pulling her against his chest, his lips pressed against her hair. "Go ahead and cry, Bet. Whatever it is, you'll feel better." He found the tip of her ear. "Don't worry," he whispered, "I have an Archie handkerchief."

The downward curve of Bet's lips climbed, and she leaned back in the circle of his arms, laughing through a haze of tears. "How dare you threaten me with that?"

Jake's broad grin betrayed his satisfaction with her change of mood. But as his eyes met hers, latching on with a sudden, startling intensity, the grin eased into the merest curve at the corners of his mouth. Even that hint of humor vanished as their eyes held, searching, probing, questioning. His fingers, meeting in the hollow of her spine, tightened, pressing and somehow possessive.

Bet experienced a feeling of déjà vu as she stared into his luminous black eyes and felt the rising tension begin to throb with a wild, primitive beat. Her heart skipped, thumped against her breastbone, and began to thunder in her ears. Some indefinable emotion flickered in his eyes—she had seen it before, but where or when had no meaning. There was only the now of a single question: What was the taste of Jake Calloway's mouth? Her palms inched across his chest, begrudging the smooth knit shirt that hugged the warmth of his skin. She broke the magnetic pull of his eyes and found his lips moving closer and closer until they blurred.

It had happened before, just like this. Her eyelashes drifted down. His heart pounded against her arms and her palms found his shoulders and her fingers touched and twined around the strong column of his neck. His mouth touched hers, velvety soft, and his hands moved across her back to fold her closer to the long, hard length of him. The kiss deepened, his mouth slanting across hers, demanding and hungry. Bet responded with an equal need that would have astonished her if she had been capable of thought. But she wasn't. She was all tingling nerve endings and pounding heart and lips... yielding... yielding... demanding...

"Jake? Bet? Is there anything I can help you with in there?" Aunt Hester's voice floated through the screen door.

Jake raised his head, his eyes unfocused, lashes at half-mast. His tongue slicked across his lips. "Bet. Ah, God, Bet," he murmured on a husk of sound.

She was the first to gather her scattered wits, though she could not summon the strength to move from his arms. "No, Mrs. March. We have everything"—the thumping lie stole her breath—"We have everything under control."

Jake's blurred gaze sharpened, and one corner of his mouth climbed his cheek. "Would you like a preview of tomorrow's headlines? 'Man Strangles Aged Aunt.'"

Bet giggled and buried her freckled nose in his chest to stifle a peal of laughter. "There's nothing funny about this, woman!" Jake protested, but she could feel his chest rippling as he began chuckling beside her ear.

She leaned back at last, knuckling her eyes, and found him watching her.

"It could be a good life, Slugger," he said softly. "What about it?"

What about it? That part of her that hoped for so much urged her to say yes, but that other part, the part that still grieved for John and their lost dreams, the part that feared more hurt, demanded that she say no. She compromised between the two, delaying the need for a decision by asking for more time. Jake's regret was obvious as he reminded her with a theatrically lascivious leer that no woman could resist him for long. If she doubted it, all she had to do was ask Aunt Hester. Shared laughter broke any lingering self-consciousness between them.

On Wednesday morning Bet found Jake at her door, bags in hand. He was on his way home. He wasn't sure how long he would be gone. His father had called about some business papers that had to be signed. His last words were "So long, Slugger," and Bet shut her door, certain she would never see him again. The day stretched out, filled with her remorse, until she returned home from work to find an earthenware crock of red roses on her doorstep. Interspersed among the roses were a wire whisk, olivewood serving spoons, cloud-shaped cookie cutters, a wooden pie crimper, and several long wooden spoons. Jake had obviously noted the wall where she hung baskets holding her kitchen utensils. She opened the card and read: *The florist thought I was crazy. Told her it was hereditary. Hoping you'll be mine—and feed me well. Jake.*

On Thursday night a basket of sweetheart roses arrived. Nestled among the roses and baby's breath was a teething ring, a rattle, and a tiny, heart-shaped brass frame with a picture of Jake. The card read: *For my best girl, Bonnie. Jake.*

Bet sighed and shifted on the stool, pressing her hands into the small of her back while she arched her shoulders. How was it possible to get used to the sound and smell and sight of a man in so short a time? So used to him that the days that had once seemed empty were as nothing to the new tomblike hush of hours that dragged from morning to dusk and back to morning.

She caught a movement out of the corner of her eye. It was Carrie, sliding off her stool to stand at the teller's window. Bet smiled to herself. She didn't need to look to know that a man had just walked through the door. While Carrie liked women, she loved men. Whether in diapers, jock straps, or support hose, a man put a twinkle in her eye and a slink in her walk.

This one must be handsome, Bet thought. Carrie had that little extra fillip of sensuality when the man was really good-looking. Long fingers patted her blatantly red hair, her hips slithered about in the confines of her skirt, her hands caressed her thighs, and she almost shivered in anticipation. Bet grinned and turned back to the pile of tens. Someone was about to get a smile to light up his day.

Ten, twenty... Carrie's husky bedroom laugh rippled ...thirty, forty, fifty... the murmur of a man's voice, low and intimate... sixty, seventy... Carrie cooed... eighty, ninety... the man laughed with a familiar sound that tingled up Bet's spine, but she reminded herself not to be foolish... one-hundred, ten, twenty... Carrie squealed, and Bet smiled... thirty, forty, fifty... Carrie's heels clicked toward her... sixty, seventy...

Long, violently violet nails tapped Bet's arm. "Honey, you been holding out on Carrie. Now, tell allll," Carrie drawled, unable to resist throwing a brilliant smile over her shoulder.

"What *allll?*" Bet drawled back.

"About that hunk asking for you!" Carrie said indignantly. She narrowed her eyes and leaned close, singsonging, "You know, the one who makes Tom Selleck look like he's got a case of the uglies."

"Jake!" Bet said, even before swiveling around to look. She was off the stool, through the swinging door, and flying across the carpeted lobby before Carrie had a chance to draw breath for further questions. Her awareness was filled by Jake, slowly straightening from his slouch against the counter, his smile spreading, a welcoming twinkle glazing his eyes.

She came to a near skidding halt a yard's distance away, suddenly conscious of the sight she must make. She'd almost thrown herself into his arms, she realized in dismay. What must he think of her? A hot blush crawled across her cheeks.

"Hi, Slugger," Jake said, sounding as though he were being strangled.

"Jake," Bet breathed, clasping her hands at her waist, her tongue numbed to further words.

"I missed you."

"I missed you, too. I—I got the flowers."

Jake stared at her, desperately scouring his mind for something to say. "Good." He could have chomped his own tongue. *Way to go, Calloway!* he castigated himself. *That ought to really impress her, you silver-tongued devil!*

Bet stared at him. "You...you took care of your business?" *You idiot!* she wailed. *He wouldn't be here if he hadn't!*

"Yes, uh..." *Damn! He was a Ph.D., not an illiterate! What happened to that quick wit and ready tongue Aunt Hester was always teasing him about?*

They yearned toward each other, swaying on firmly planted feet.

God, she's beautiful!

Mrs. March is right. He's gorgeous!

She's perfect!

He's perfect!

Carrie, draped across the counter, rolled her eyes toward the misty purple shadow beneath her finely plucked brows and did a drumroll on the countertop with her fingernails. "Hey, handsome! What'cha doing standing there? Ask her out to lunch! A dollar to a doughnut, she'll go."

Bet straightened with a snap of her spine. "Oh! How rude of me! Carrie, this is Jake Calloway. Jake, this is my best friend, Carrie Brewster."

"Pleased to meetcha." Carrie grinned.

"Ms. Brewster," Jake nodded, unable to tear his eyes from Bet. "Will you have lunch with me?"

"Yes, I'd love to. I'll just have to get—"

At that moment the door opened, letting in a blast of summery heat. Bet's eyes strayed toward it. Oh, no! Not now! Her stomach coiled in a tight, nauseating knot, and she edged toward Jake, sliding her hand into the crook of his arm.

Jake sensed her sudden tension and saw the slight quiver in the smile she gave the woman who approached with a long-legged, purposeful stride. He noted the woman's gaunt face lined with discontentment and knew that, whoever she was, he wasn't going to like her.

"Mrs. Valentine, I'm—I'm surprised to see you here today," Bet said hesitantly.

"I've asked you to call me Nancy," she said crisply. Blue eyes as sharp as dagger points flashed toward Jake, then pierced Bet. "I need to speak to you. Privately."

"Mrs. . . . Nancy, I'd like for you to meet—"

"I'm not interested in meeting one of your men. Is the conference room in use?"

"One of my . . ." Breath failed Bet, and her fingers dug into Jake's arm.

He covered her hand with his, giving it a comforting squeeze. "My name is Jake Calloway, Mrs. Valentine. I'm a friend of Bet's." He emphasized *friend* with the hint of a threat.

Nancy Valentine's nostrils flared away from the blade-like bridge of her nose, but she ignored him. "Is the conference room in use?"

Bet swallowed anger and humiliation, something she had done often when dealing with John's mother. "No, it isn't. Jake?" Beseeching eyes pleaded with him, and he nodded, following as she led the way.

The conference room was a bare-bones room with dark paneling, a thick, rust-colored carpet, a round table circled by chairs, and an empty easel in one corner. Jake seated Bet, one hand resting on her tense shoulder in a gesture that told her she was not alone, before he took a seat beside her. She gave him a grateful smile that trembled at the corners, and he frowned at Nancy Valentine. Brittle around the edges, he thought, and knew that Bet was too vulnerable to have dealt with this woman on anything but the rockiest terms. His gaze moved to Bet. Her eyes were too wide, too still. Her shoulders were squared for battle, and Jake began to wonder. John Valentine. What had he been like? Had he protected Bet from his mother?

Nancy Valentine riffled through her briefcase, withdrawing legal papers and a pen, which she shoved across the width of the table. "Sign at the crosses."

"What are these?" Bet asked cautiously.

"The lawsuits against the driver and the owner of the dump truck that killed my son."

Bet slid the papers back with a single finger, as though they were distasteful to her. "I told you, I will have no part of this."

"I'm suing in Bonnie's name. You have to sign as her legal guardian." Thin fingers shoved the papers back toward Bet.

"We've been over this again and again." Bet sighed in frustration. "It was an accident. The man's brakes failed. There is no one to blame, and I won't take blood money in my name or Bonnie's for an accident that was no one's fault! Don't you think the driver of that truck feels guilty enough without our hounding him with a lawsuit?"

Her mother-in-law's pale face suffused with rage. "He can never feel guilty enough for murdering my son! With you or without you, I intend to ruin him!"

"Then you'll do it without me."

"Very well." Nancy Valentine scooped up the papers, slammed the briefcase shut, and snapped the latches. "Have you asked for your promotion yet?" she barked suddenly.

"No, there are no openings."

"I told you not to wait!" Her thin hand slammed down on the briefcase. "You'll never get anywhere if you don't let them know you're interested! How do you expect to support Bonnie or set the right example for her if you don't work at it? A young girl *needs* the good example of a strong woman today!"

Bet flinched, and Jake's temper began to simmer.

"I will never understand why my son married you! You ruined him! He needed a strong woman! One who would—"

Jake's fist thudded on the table, bringing the tirade to an abrupt halt. He leaned forward, glittering black eyes narrowed to slits. "You are talking to the woman I intend to marry. Say another word against her at your own risk!"

"Is this true?"

Dagger points of blue again sliced at Bet, and for once she didn't squirm beneath that hostile stare. She didn't even notice it. In all of her life, no one had ever taken up for her. John had often apologized for his mother after the fact, but he never opposed her for Bet's sake. Warmth curled around her heart. All she could see was Jake. Jake watching her. Jake waiting with anger still clouding his eyes. Jake . . .

She smiled, a tentative smile. "Yes," she said quietly, and her smile grew, bright, happy, eager. "Yes, it's true."

Jake's smile matched her own as he drew her hand to his lips. "It will be a good life, Slugger," he promised huskily.

Although a hectic week passed, it seemed to Bet she no sooner said yes than her wedding day arrived. Feeling more than a little harried, she stood in the parlor of the old high-ceilinged farmhouse trying to match the familiar names of Jake's family members with unfamiliar faces. Somehow the pictures hadn't helped at all. His brothers, Pete and Burt, were as alike as twins. Which of them went with plump, smiling Terry and which went with thin, unsmiling Marlene was a mystery to her. As for the seven nephews and nieces mingling with an assortment of small cousins, sorting them out was a hopeless task best saved for later.

The Calloways, their relatives and their neighbors were huggers, and Bet was beginning to feel battered, bruised, and more than a little frightened. But Jake stayed at her side, making the introductions, a possessive and comforting hand at her waist. Unfortunately, her attention was sorely divided between all those new faces and her attempt to keep an eye on Bonnie, who was being passed from hand to hand. Her cheeks began to tire from maintaining a fixed smile, and her eyes were glazing over when she felt a hand on her arm.

Jake's mother smiled up at her. "The preacher called to say he'll be delayed awhile. You look a little ragged, Bet. Would you like to freshen up?"

"Bonnie?" she asked anxiously, unwilling to let her daughter out of her sight.

"I'll bring her." Jake leaned down, shouting above a decibel level that was reaching that of a rock concert.

Bet followed his mother into the hall, sighing when they closed the door behind them. The silence was deafening and more than welcome to Bet's frazzled nerves. She would have relaxed and enjoyed it, if she hadn't been alone with Jake's mother for the first time. She had embarked on her first marriage prepared to love John's parents as she loved him. It had been a shock to find herself actively resented by Nancy Valentine, who never lost an opportunity to sideswipe the shaky legs of Bet's self-confidence. Bet determined not to open herself up to that hurt this time. If the hand of friendship was offered, she would accept it, gladly. But she wouldn't expect it.

The bedroom was huge, with broad double windows covered by sheer curtains through which she could see the lower limbs of the redbud tree with its fragile, heart-shaped leaves. Her purse and Bonnie's diaper bag lay atop the hand-crocheted spread of the sturdy pine bed. It was a room with a lived-in simplicity that she would have loved at any other time. Now she scarcely noticed it as she hovered in the doorway, tamping down a strong urge to cut and run.

Esther Calloway sank into one of the two rockers set on a large braided rug. "Have a seat, Bet. You look tuckered out."

"It—it's been a long day, and it"—she swallowed hard—"it isn't over yet." She edged toward the other rocker, then sat, with her feet tightly crossed at the ankles and her hands twined together in her lap. Her gaze strayed toward the door, and she prayed silently that Jake would come soon.

"He'll be along in a minute," Esther said, as though

she had read Bet's mind. "I expect somebody collared him and slowed him down. I'm glad. This will give us a chance to talk."

Bet's heart sank. She knew all about mother-in-law—daughter-in-law talks. "Yes, ma'am."

"Are you afraid of me, Bet?"

"Oh, no!" Her wide eyes flew to Esther Calloway's face. Except for the absence of glasses and a more peaceful expression in her blue eyes, Jake's mother was a replica of Mrs. March, whom Bet loved dearly. But Mrs. March was a friend, while this woman was a stranger, soon to be her mother-in-law. Her gaze fell, and she swallowed the lump of fear in her throat. "Yes, ma'am," she admitted painfully.

"There's no reason to be. I've yet to bite either of my son's wives, and I can see no reason to start with you." That comment was so much like Mrs. March it brought the ghost of a smile to Bet's mouth. "However, I do believe we should be truthful with one another. I cannot tell you I approve of this marriage, and I must admit I've done everything I could to persuade Jake against it."

Bet's stricken gaze raised.

"It has nothing to do with you, dear. Hester has the very highest opinion of you, and I would welcome you with open arms, if you and Jake loved each other. You are a mother, Bet, so you can understand a mother's wish that her child marry where he is loved."

"Yes, ma'am. I can understand that." Tears pricked at Bet's eyelids. No matter that she refused to expect too much; she had hoped for a great deal.

A hand covered hers, patting gently. She looked up to meet Esther Calloway's kindly gaze. "Jake is a grown man. When I cannot influence him, I accept his decisions, as I will accept you—with a whole heart. I only tell you this because I wouldn't want you to hear of my objections from someone else. My interest is my son's happiness, and I trust him enough to believe he knows his own mind."

"Do you think he does? Everything happened so fast,

Mrs. Calloway. And Jake is so . . ." She looked up with shimmering eyes. "He's so forceful! I wonder if we haven't made a terrible mistake!" Her voice rose on a high note of uncertainty.

"Mom?" There was an odd note, almost like a warning, in Jake's voice as he stood in the doorway, Bonnie wriggling up and down on his shoulder. "I wouldn't want Bet to be upset."

The odd emphasis of warning penetrated the bubbling doubt that infected Bet. She started violently, staring at Jake with dismay. "Please, your mother has been very kind to me. It's just that . . . we . . . this is wrong, Jake! It's wrong!"

Jake flung a furious look at his mother, who shook her head, murmuring, "Wedding-day jitters."

"Here, Mom, Bonnie's wet." While his mother laid Bonnie on the bed and began searching through the diaper bag, Jake went to Bet. He knelt before her and cupped her clenched fists in the cradle of his hands. "Tell me," he urged quietly.

She couldn't speak past the lump that was growing ever larger in her throat. She could only stare at him with wide, terrified eyes while the soft, silky autumn-gold bow at her throat rose and fell with her rapid breaths. She saw the shock of thick black hair waving away from the widow's peak that dipped into his sun-browned forehead. A slight frown drew his heavy, wide-spaced eyebrows together. Beneath them, his eyes held an expression of watchful patience. Even now, at his most serious, the corners of his beautiful mouth teased with the promise of a smile. His chin was squared off, blending into an uncompromising jawline. It was the face of a stranger.

Bet drew a shuddering breath. "We don't know each other," she whispered wildly.

His hands tightened around hers, the thumbs caressing lightly. "Go on."

"What . . . what if you don't like me after you get to know me?" Not even to herself would Bet admit why that question burst from her.

"That won't happen. How could you think it would?" She stared at him helplessly, ensnared by his tender gaze. A question sprang into his eyes. The lush black lashes narrowed, and his mouth thinned to a grim line. "Bet, are you thinking about your mother?"

A small breath of shocked surprise puffed at her lips, and the pricking tears flooded her eyes. She straightened self-consciously but could not find the strength to break the gently questioning tether of his eyes. "She . . . she didn't want me, you know," she said almost primly.

His hands convulsed around hers in a painful grip. "But I do! I need you, and I want you, Slugger," he said softly. "This is right. I know it is."

"Are you su—" She blinked as another thought intruded. "Do you really need me, Jake?"

His lips curled into a soft smile. "I'm going to have a hard time having babies without you, Slugger. And now that I've met you, somehow I can't imagine having them with anyone else."

"I . . . I'm afraid," she whispered.

"So am I." Her expression of surprise drew a chuckle from him. "I want you to be happy, Bet. This may not be our great romance, but it can grow into something strong and lasting. I want that."

"So do I. More than anything."

"Then marry me, Slugger. I need you."

"It is right, isn't it?" she breathed.

"It's more right than either of you know," Esther Calloway announced with a touch of dry humor. Both Jake and Bet had forgotten she was in the room. They looked up with equally startled expressions to see her holding Bonnie and smiling down at them. "I don't think you need it, but I'd like to give you my blessing. Bet, both Terry and Marlene call me Mother Calloway. I hope you will, too."

"Moth . . ." Bet bit her trembling lip. "I'd like that."

Jake stood, enveloped his mother in a bear hug, and laughed. "I told you you'd love her." He turned to Bet, taking her hand and pulling her out of the rocker. "C'mon, woman. I don't think I can wait any longer, and I hear a car driving up. That ought to be the preacher."

It wasn't. Carrie Brewster breezed into the crowded parlor like a gaudy peacock strutting through a yard full of drab brown hens. She wore a royal purple suit with a brilliant red blouse that clashed horribly with her startling red hair. Bet had never seen a more welcome sight.

"Sugar, I'm so sorry I'm late. I've trailed dust on every gravel road between here and Shreveport. Thought I'd never find the right one!" She threw her arms around Bet, enfolding her in a smothering cloud of perfume, and promptly burst into tears. "I miss you already," she wailed. "Oh, look at that! I almost knocked your hat off!" She straightened the white felt hat with its small upturned brim, smoothing a lock of Bet's bronze hair. "And I got lipstick on you!" She rubbed at the violet-red smear on Bet's cheek and flung an angry look at Jake. "I sure hope you know how lucky you are, Jake Calloway! There ain't many women like Bet, and you better take good care of her!"

"I do, I know, and I will." He grinned, dodging Bonnie's small fist.

"You just better! Ohhh!" She burst into renewed tears. "Married, Bet! You're getting married! Oh, I'm so happy!"

In the hubbub, the preacher arrived. Minutes later the wedding party was arranged in the bright patch of light pouring through the double windows leading to the screened porch. Bet stood, feeling small and pale in her white linen suit, beside Jake, who insisted on holding Bonnie. His liquid gaze embraced them both. "When she's older, I want Bonnie to know that I wanted her as much as I wanted her mother. We'll be a family, Bet."

At that moment Bet Valentine knew she was the most fortunate woman in the world. She was touched too deeply for tears, but an aching tenderness welled up inside her. She rested one trembling hand on Jake's arm and smiled up at him. "A family," she said reverently.

As the ceremony progressed, it was accompanied by

the strange sounds of gulping, sniffling, sighing, and outright sobbing from Carrie, who was acting as Bet's maid of honor. Bonnie discovered Jake's mouth, and tiny fingers wormed through his lips. His "I do" was muffled by the four fingers clamped firmly over his lower teeth. He detached them and began searching his pocket. As he withdrew an Archie handkerchief, Bet's "I do" came out in a chirruping laugh. Their eyes met briefly with that shared memory, and Jake shook out the handkerchief in all its garish glory, handing it to Carrie.

"I now pronounce you husband and wife" was drowned out by Carrie's awed "My Gawd!"

NEW BEGINNINGS

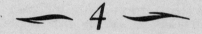

A COOL BREEZE carried the swishing music of pine needles into the darkened bedroom of Jake's ranch-style house, where Bet huddled beneath the covers watching Jake's dark shadow shed his clothes. Her haunted gaze fled that sight, turning to the low windows. In the distance, twinkling through the pine thicket, she could see the lights burning in the old farmhouse, where Bonnie lay sleeping in the crib that had been used by Jake and his brothers. It had been less than an hour since she gave her daughter a last kiss and wrung a promise from Jake's mother to call if she were needed, but she felt it had been eons and knew a desperate desire to have her daughter nearby tonight. One light winked out, then another. The house was dark, the night brightened only by the glaze of moonlight. Bet shivered and felt the bed sink with the weight of her new husband. Oh, dear God! What had she done?

"Your hands are like ice," Jake murmured, pulling them to his chest and warming them with one hand while he braced himself on an elbow over her. "Are you afraid, Bet?"

"Yes."

"I won't hurt you. I'll never hurt you." His husky whisper washed over her. "Relax. You laughed with me today. Remember? You weren't afraid then; there's no reason for you to be now. Share yourself with me, Bet. Share yourself, and this can be beautiful."

His voice soothed and his lips teased until hers softened, parting for his kiss. His hand touched her shoulder, the callused thumb resting at the hollow of her throat, where her terrified pulse throbbed. His mouth slanted across hers, firm yet achingly gentle, and her throbbing pulse began to slow.

Tension seeped from Bet. The wiry black hair on Jake's chest tickled her warming hands, and she felt the heavy thud of his heart against her palms. Silk and lace, a frothy creation that revealed more than it concealed, caressed her with fragility while Jake's fingers eased the thin strap down her arm. The moist heat of his breath played across her chin and down her neck. She felt the pressure of his lips and the teasing rasp of his beard-stubbled cheek and the slight trembling of his palm drifting down her shoulder and across the mound of her breast to cup the strangely yearning peak.

Pleasure scampered along her nerves, trailing a languid heat, and Bet arched into his palm and heard the breathless shudder of her name. His mouth claimed hers with a sudden edge of desperation, and the muscled length of his forearm pressed against her waist, drawing her closer, molding her to the heated length of him. The hard bulge of his manhood burned her thigh, and a growing, aching need kindled in the core of her being.

A single tear trickled across Bet's temple. It would all be over soon. She would be left with that ache dully throbbing its question: What would it be like to have it assuaged? What would it be like, just once, to know?

"Bet," Jake murmured against her lips, "I want to touch you. All of you."

His hands were magic, sprinkling intoxicating bursts

of heat as they eased her straps down her arms and slid
the slippery silk down...down. The gentle strength of
his dark hands encompassed her ribs and cupped her
breasts. The tips of his fingers traced ribbons of fire
across her abdomen and stroked the pale gold of her
quivering thighs before he tossed the cloud of white silk
into the darkness. Moonlight glistened across his hair
and gleamed in his eyes, and Bet waited...
waited...watching while he bent low. His lips nestled
against her ankle, and a shock sprayed through her leg.
Breath hissed sharply into her constricted lungs.

All attempts at thought were abandoned for pure feeling. There was no grief for yesterday, no worry for tomorrow, only the now of screaming nerve endings
centered about the questing lips that rained fire around
her sensitive knees, climbing...climbing...

"No, no!" Bet tangled her hands in Jake's thick hair.

His soft sigh of regret caressed her as he moved up,
covering her body with his. He toyed with her lips, nibbling, tugging. His tongue delved into the corners of her
mouth, tracing the bow of her upper lip and sliding across
the lower, teasing without mercy until Bet could stand
no more. Her grasping fingers cupped his head, dragging
his mouth hard against hers. Aching and fear and wonder
were but a frothy mist as her knees began to yield. His
hips caressed her inner thighs. Heat touched and probed,
sweetly, ah, so sweetly, filling her with the pulsating
strength that was Jake Calloway.

"Bet, Bet," he groaned against her shoulder, "I need
you. I need you."

Deep within her a tight knot of apprehension unrav-
eled. It was enough to be needed, to be wanted, to share
her loneliness with this lonely man. Her small hand curled
across his nape, her lips brushed his cheek, and she felt
his smile before his lips began to cherish hers with wild
abandon.

He moved in long, leisurely strokes that spun slowly
to the edge of time and crept back, wooing Bet with the

promise of fulfillment. Her eyes flew wide, and she met his gaze, seeing there a shining wonder that matched her own.

"Together, Bet. Together, always."

"Always," she answered, and she felt the leaping response of his body. Pleasure burgeoned to pain and blossomed into an exquisite flower of ecstasy that flung her into a rainbow sky of brilliant, smiling colors. She heard him cry her name and felt him shudder and knew they had shared of themselves and it was good. Her fingers trailed across the straining muscles of his back, and she smiled, a languorous smile of repletion. Their children would be born of beauty if not of love, and she was content.

Jake nuzzled her neck, the hot, harsh gasps of his breath slowing gradually. "I never dreamed, Bet...I never dreamed..." The word sighed into uncertainty, and he raised himself up, his elbows propped on the pillows, his hands cradling her face. "It *is* right, Slugger."

"Yes." She smiled and drew his head down to give him the benediction of a kiss.

It was the moonlight that woke her. A silvered strip that probed the treetops and sneaked through the window to drape itself across her face. It was the moonlight, she insisted to herself. Not that deadening weight of guilt that trod heavily through her restless sleep. She stared at the tousled black head sharing her pillow and felt the prickling of tears. A sob gathered beneath her breastbone, pressing painfully against her throat. She clenched her teeth, swallowing hard.

She eased away and reached down to move the hand that lay curled upon her waist. It was warm to her touch, and she cupped her palm across the knuckles and rubbed his fingers lightly, feeling the tiny tufts of hair. A glimmer of a smile pulled the sadness from her drooping lips. There was no fear in her now, nor would there ever be again. Jake Calloway was a man born to tenderness. She envied his Tricia, who had known that tenderness coupled with love.

She slipped from the bed, gently lowering his hand to the mattress. A streak of moonlight lay across his discarded terry-cloth robe, and Bet snatched it up as she padded quietly from the room. A dull glow brightened the end of the long hall where she entered the sprawling, cathedral-ceilinged area that was living room, kitchen, and dining room all in one. She moved toward the glass wall that arched high overhead and sank down to stare out into the night.

The sob was there again, pushing up with a pressure equal to her desire to suppress it. Like a sharp-edged rock it sat in her chest, the pain of it flooding her eyes with tears. Wondering fingers trailed across her lips and lightly traced the abrasions at the corners of her mouth caused by Jake's bristles. The thought of him brought a rush of breathtaking warmth to her loins, and the sob fought its way out of her throat. She pressed her hands to her tingling breasts, flattening them with unrelenting pressure.

What had happened to her? It was wrong! Wrong! Everything was wrong! Why Jake? Why not John? She had loved John. She had worshiped him. Yet he had never done anything more than ruffle the surface of a passion Jake had taken and molded to his own pattern.

Feature by feature, she fought to build John's face. The sensitive, gentle mouth. The sad, lonely eyes. The square jaw that was more stubborn than firm. Her life with him had been one of calm serenity, a serenity she needed desperately after the upheavals of her childhood. John had been everything she wanted in a man. Patient, kind, thoughtful. Everything!

Turmoil scattered Bet's thoughts in a ragged crazy quilt as Jake's bold, dark face overlaid that of John's. It was Jake with his liquid black eyes and melodic deep voice that carried her with him to the rapturous heights.

Jake who sparked the dormant fires of her passion. Jake who imprinted himself on her soul by her body's possession. It was wrong! There was no love between them, yet . . . yet it was beautiful. How could anything so wrong feel so right? How could it stir her to the depths of her being and leave her with the certainty that she was born to . . .

Bet's head sank into her hands, and she wept her confusion while the tearing guilt gnawed at her. Somehow she had betrayed John and his memory.

Her head raised slowly, dull eyes lifting blindly to the night. One hand splayed across the cool glass, and she searched for the moon peeking through the feathery tops of the pines.

"John, John, why did you leave me?"

Jake woke slowly with a delicious, languorous ease. He stretched until his bones cracked, scratched at his chest, ruffled his hair, and grinned at the cool elegance of a shaft of moonlight that bathed his face. Lord, he couldn't remember when he had felt so good! Just why eluded him at the moment, and he was too sluggish to give it much thought. He gave himself up to that heavenly relaxation, a smile of utter peace curling his mouth.

Bet, he thought lazily. That was it. Who would have ever dreamed that one wisp of a sensible woman could drive him wild? Of all the things he had expected from their marriage, that was a surprising bonus.

"Aunt Hester, old girl," he whispered with an idiotic grin, "there'll be something special under your tree come Christmas."

He sighed and stretched out his hand, reached farther, and his head whipped around on the pillow. She was gone! He sat up, staring around the room. Nothing! She couldn't . . . she wouldn't . . .

His bare feet slapped quietly on the oak floor. He found her in the den, curled up before the glass wall that looked out into the copse of pines. She was a figure sculpted in moonlight and shadows and loneliness, and

Jake found himself caught in the strange timelessness of the moment.

Anxiety died. She was there; she was his. The fullness of that knowledge swelled his heart with a curious humbling pride. He had never known a woman like Bet. He didn't understand how she could be so vulnerable yet so open and loving. He found himself wanting to protect her, to give her the happiness she had been denied for so long. He thought of Tricia and felt the easing of the tie that bound him to her. Tricia would not begrudge him this new happiness. She would have agreed with Aunt Hester, who'd had three husbands and loved them all to distraction. A smile slipped easily into place as he watched Bet's head rise and her hand lift to the glass. He took a step forward.

"John, John, why did you leave me?"

It was a poignant, wistful sigh filled with weary hopelessness; a question that burrowed into Jake's heart with needling pain. He hung there for a moment, then turned away, vanishing into the dark tunnel of the hall to seek his empty bed and try to banish the numbing feeling that something infinitely precious had slipped through his fingers.

Sleep was long in coming; and when morning arrived with the cheerful trilling of a bird, Jake woke with a jerk that pulled him from the bed. He was alone, still! Pausing long enough to yank on his jeans to a steady stream of cursing, he barreled down the hall with dread dogging his every step. He burst into the living room and saw Bet curled up on the floor before the glass wall. Her name died on his lips as he skidded to a halt. His toe connected with the corner of the rattan magazine rack sitting beside his favorite chair.

"Damn!" he shouted, clutching his toe and hopping around on one foot.

Bet sat up, blinking the sleep from her eyes. Suddenly her blurred gaze connected with a furious black stare. "Jake, what—"

"I stubbed my toe! Damn!" He lowered his foot and tested his weight on it, wriggling his toe up and down while his thoughts raced. It wouldn't do any good to mention the odd fact that she was sleeping on the floor. Besides, he might hear more of her reason than he wanted to. "Guess I'll live." He grinned, hobbling over to Bet and offering her his hand. "C'mon, woman. We've got places to go and things to do, and the day's half-gone. You city slickers might sleep the day away, but in the country we get up with the rooster's crow."

"When is that?" Bet asked as he pulled her up with one smooth yank.

"Dawn."

"Dawn!" She stared at him aghast. "Is it too late for an annulment?"

"Hell, yes! You can't tell me you forgot..." Jake thought better of it, his eyes moving uneasily away from Bet's burning blush. "Why don't you go on and get cleaned up. I'll put on the coffee."

She left him without a word, nearly running down the hall. Jake watched her, a frown thundering across his brow while his hands curled into fists. There was no need for humor when she couldn't see him. He moved slowly into the kitchen, ignoring the stinging pain in his toe. Dragging out the coffee, he paused to listen to the faint sound of the shower. He wasn't a masochist. He would give Bet what she wanted and no more. It would be a good life filled with kindness, affection, and the shared love of their children. It *would*, he insisted, but a bleak light dulled his eyes.

A board creaked as Bet flew across the back porch a step ahead of Jake, who had challenged her to a race. She slapped the door frame and turned around with a triumphant laugh. "Beat ya!"

"You cheated!" he protested, standing on the steps and rubbing his stomach. "It was all those pancakes you fed me. Lord, woman! If I'd known you could cook like that, I wouldn't have wasted these two weeks!"

"Is it my fault you made a hog of yourself?"

His eyes sparkled mischievously. "I'm just a growing boy."

"Ha! Two batches of pancakes every morning and you'll be growing out, not up. C'mon, I feel as if I haven't seen Bonnie in ages!"

She hurried through the door and stopped with a gasping laugh. Bonnie lay in her carrier atop the huge round table covered with a plaid-patterned vinyl cloth. Her strawberry curls were plastered to her head with a mixture of Pablum and Gerber's mashed plums. There was a dollop of plums on her knee and Pablum between her toes and fingers. When she caught sight of Bet, she gave a toothless grin and blew a spray of Pablum bubbles.

"I should have warned you," Bet cried as her father-in-law swiveled around on his chair, picking Pablum from his eyebrows. "Bonnie likes to play with her food."

"I noticed." He grinned that infectious smile his son had inherited.

Bonnie gurgled and squirmed and kicked at the tiny spoon Mr. Calloway held, sending a shower of plums raining into his white hair and dribbling down his forehead. Bet shrieked and jumped forward but was too late.

"I'm so sorry," she said, raising her hand to her mouth to hide her smile. He didn't look much cleaner than Bonnie, and there was a real question as to just how much had actually made it into her daughter's mouth. "Would you like for me to finish feeding her?"

He scrubbed his forehead and laughed. "Heck, no! This young lady and I are coming to an understanding. Aren't we, sweet'en?" he cooed. Bonnie wrapped a sticky hand around his finger and opened her mouth as he aimed the spoon at it. "You tell your mama that you and Grandpa are getting along just fine." He nodded his head up and down, and Bonnie watched him, enthralled. She smiled a tentative smile that turned into a squeal and tried to nod like he did.

Bet felt Jake's arm slide around her waist, pulling her against him. "Well, Dad, what do you think of my two girls?"

Jason Calloway's eyes met Bet's briefly with a kindly twinkle. "I think you're a lucky devil. Welcome to the Calloway clan, Bet. I hope you'll be happy with us."

"Thank you." She looked away, unable to say more for fear of bursting into tears. This was what it was like to belong to a family. This feeling of comfort, of belonging, of acceptance. Bonnie would never have to suffer for the lack of those things. Grandpa! He wanted her to call him Grandpa, just as if she really belonged to him!

"Bet, dear!"

"Mrs. March, good morning."

"Mrs. March? What's this? I'm Aunt Hester now."

Bet's lip trembled, and she bit it. Her cup was overflowing. "Aunt Hester," she said softly, hugging the older woman. Her eyes rose, and she saw her mother-in-law hurrying into the kitchen. "Mother Calloway," she whispered tentatively, unsure whether she should really call her that.

Esther Calloway smiled readily. "Morning, Bet. Have you had breakfast?"

"Have we!" Jake laughed. "Mom, Bet makes pancakes like nobody's I've ever tasted!"

Bet flushed slightly, casting an anxious glance at her mother-in-law. It was something short of diplomatic to praise a new wife's cooking to a mother. She had learned that quickly with Nancy Valentine, whose hackles rose whenever John praised Bet.

"Bet, you'll have to share your recipe with me. As long as there's a lot of it, Jake could eat shoe leather and never know the difference. It's high praise indeed, if he noticed."

Bet relaxed with a relieved smile. This wasn't going to be the same at all. Everything was different. Everything was perfect! She gave Jake a dazzling smile and slipped her hand into his.

"Now, ya'll run along. One day isn't much of a honeymoon, but we'll take good care of Bonnie."

"She isn't too much trouble, is she?"

"Lands, child! She's a lamb. Don't you worry about a thing."

"Let's go, Bet. I want to show you the place," Jake said, urging her toward the door.

As they stepped onto the porch, closing the door behind them, Aunt Hester's cheery voice floated out. "I told you, Esther. Didn't I tell you? It's a match made in heaven!"

Bet's tawny gaze widened, clashing with Jake's before it fled with self-condemning haste. In that brief contact she saw a flare of surprise and a dimming expression of withdrawal. The laughter and ease they had found were gone in the blink of an eye. A match made in heaven. But it wasn't! It was a match made on earth for earthly reasons. They would never know the ecstasy of two people who had discovered in each other all the things that complement and expand their own unique individuality. There would never be the heartrending rapture of romantic love. They were two practical people embarked on a practical marriage. It was what she wanted. It was!

They passed a cluster of small buildings, strolled along the fenced-in chicken yard, and walked around a huge garden with neat rows of growing vegetables. Jake talked steadily, pointing out paddocks with horses and a distant field where Brahmans and Herefords grazed beneath rows of tall pecan trees.

The substance of what he said was lost on Bet, who was listening to the sound of his voice. The deep melodic tone held a distance that was new to Bet. She stumbled over a clump of grass, and Jake's hand was at her elbow, but the moment she caught her balance he released her and moved a step away. The drone of his voice took on an even more aloof quality, and Bet's heart sank to the toes of her tennis shoes.

She could hear his every quiet footfall, the swish of his jeans and the slight crackling of his starched cotton shirt. She darted a glance at his hand and found it drawn into a tight fist that swung awkwardly at his side. Reluctantly she looked up at his face. As though drawn by the power of her gaze, he stopped, his liquid black eyes staring deep into hers. It was then that she realized he was as aware of her as she was of him. Aware that she was a woman as he was a man. Aware of honeyed feminine flesh and dark masculine skin. Aware of softness and hardness, curves and hollows. Aware, until the knowledge was a sizzling cauldron in the brain.

She fought the hypnotic pull of his eyes and looked down at her tightly clasped hands. "It . . . it doesn't matter, Jake," she murmured.

"Doesn't it?"

"Aunt . . . Aunt Hester is a romantic. She wants to think . . . but—but we know it isn't true." She chanced a peek and was snared. "Don't we?" she asked, unaware of the fragile tracery of pleading.

His burning eyes delved deep into hers, and Bet hung suspended on that probing question. Suddenly he whirled, striding away with long, rapid steps that forced her to run after him.

"The stable is this way." Every word was edged with ice that slipped beneath Bet's skin like slivers.

She explored the stalls, fingered the bridles, and petted a new foal who stalked about with a stiff-legged wobbly gait. And all the while Jake leaned against a rough-hewn column, arms crossed over his chest, dark eyes following her every move until she wanted to run screaming from the tension that raked like sharp claws along her nerves.

She didn't know this man with his frowning face and tightly curled lips. She didn't like the anger she could feel simmering within him. She was afraid, but the fear could not quench the leap of anticipation whenever his dark eyes met hers with a smoky promise.

They left the stables without touching, without talking. A breeze rippled the hay field into an undulating sea of green as they left the lingering acrid odor of the stables behind. A barn climbed toward the powder-puff sky, its doors yawning wide. Beside it was a tall sweet gum tree shading a large flatbed wagon and a tractor. Bet's eyes moved back toward the chasm beyond those open doors. She felt the prickle of . . . what? Fear? Hesitation? Premonition? She couldn't decide what it was. She only knew that her feet dragged to a halt.

Jake paused a few steps ahead of her. Sunlight slanting through the tree brightened the solemnity of his face. His sober stare sent a shiver of apprehension through Bet.

"It's too late for that," he said quietly, raising his hand.

One dragging step. Their fingers touched; their hands meshed. His was warm; hers, cold and trembling. She licked her dry lips, eyes wide with the knowledge that she would not be able to turn away from him, even if she wanted to. And she didn't! It was damning but undeniable. She wanted to know where he would lead her. She wanted to know what he would do. She wanted to yield to the anticipation that leaped like darting flames through her veins. She wanted to experience the promise in his eyes.

The summer heat died in the cool shade within the barn. The smell of dust and hay was in the air. Cobwebs draped the corners, and a ladder led to the loft. She climbed it slowly, step by step. Jake followed. At the top Bet turned to watch him step onto the rough plank flooring. He came to her. The earth stood still and waited breathlessly.

He didn't move or touch her. He just stood and stared with a curiously expressionless face. But Bet sensed the turmoil that raged behind the darkling depths of his eyes. A turmoil that matched her own. Was he feeling the same things? That kaleidoscope of careening emotions— guilt, fear, desire—until she didn't know which was uppermost: her need to retain her crisp, clear image of her first husband or her need to reach out for a new life with this one.

When he moved at last, she flinched. His hand hovered inches from her face, pain leaped into his eyes, and his skin paled. Slowly his hand lowered to hang loose at his side. Without a word he stepped around her, going to the open loft door.

Bet watched his measured steps. She saw him framed in sunlight. She saw the rise and fall of his shoulders as he drew long, deep breaths, and she knew she had hurt him. How, she wasn't sure. It wasn't as if their every word or gesture was evaluated with the sensitizing emotion of love.

She took a faltering step. Would it be better to go to him or to leave him alone? She didn't know him well enough to be sure, but the sight of him bathed in sunlight and solitude was more than she could stand. She touched his arm and felt it quiver beneath her fingers.

"Jake?"

"Yes."

"I—I'm sorry."

"Don't be." He continued to stare out at the grassy field broken by a rutted wagon track. "I'm expecting too much, too fast. It's my problem, Bet, not yours."

Her hand tightened around his arm. The flesh quivered beneath her touch once again, and she heard the ragged sigh of his breath and saw the thick brush of his lashes flutter over his eyes. "You're wrong," she said softly. "You're my husband. We should share more than—than—"

"Sex," he volunteered dryly, still not looking at her.

The whisper of a wounded breath hissed through her lips, and she released him, stepping back and swiveling away so he could not see the sudden sparkle of tears that welled in her eyes. *Sex*. It sounded so cold, so calculated, so empty. What they shared had been so much more than that!

"Bet, I'm sorry," he said, so close his breath ruffled a lock of her hair. "I'm in a rotten mood, and I shouldn't take it out on you."

She drew a shaky breath and tried to laugh. "I thought that was what wives were for."

"Dammit!" Jake pulled her around and stopped suddenly, staring down into her tear-flooded eyes. "Bet! Dear God, Bet," he said huskily, "don't look at me like that." As though the lure of her trembling lips was more than he could resist, he leaned down and molded his mouth to hers with gentle persuasion. "Don't cry. I promise I'll never be angry again."

Bet twined her arms around his neck and leaned back with a sad, amused smile. "Don't make promises neither of us can keep. I warn you, I can be a perfect shrew when the mood takes me."

"I don't believe it."

"The more fool you." Her shimmering golden gaze held his, her smile fading with the leap of passion that turned his black eyes smoky. Anticipation licked at the pit of her stomach, and Bet melted into his savage kiss, welcoming the crushing strength of his arms.

He lifted her, holding her tight against his chest, as he carried her to the corner of the loft. She felt the sharp tickling of scattered bits of straw and smelled dust and watched him lean over her. His dark face and hot eyes blurred, his lips touched hers, and thought splintered into radiating shards that were crushed into the powder of mindlessness.

Clothes were peeled off in trembling haste and popping buttons. One small red tennis shoe left Jake's hand like a projectile, sailing through the open loft door; the other found a nest atop a pyramid of hay bales. His boot skidded across the rough floor and tumbled to the ground with a dull, unnoticed thud. They strove together with a furied passion at its most primitive; a striving for union that would not be denied. Every touch blistered. Every kiss inflamed. Every moaning word of need and desire was sucked deep into the whirling vortex that enthralled them.

When it was over and they lay gasping for breath, Bet sat up with wide, horrified eyes. Her scream of fulfillment rang in her ears. The violence of her response was scored into Jake's body with reddening nail marks. Nausea clutched at her. She didn't know herself anymore. Love wasn't like this! Love was soft and tender and sedate. Love was . . . dull.

Oh, God! How could she think that? Her hands covered her eyes. She was going crazy! Her fingers inched down her cheeks, and her eyes reluctantly met Jake's. A chill crawled over her skin. His black eyes were bright with a horror to equal her own.

His lashes dropped like shutters. "Did—did I hurt you, Bet?"

"I—I don't think so."

"I don't know what . . ."

But he did know what had come over him. Lust and love and fury. He would have murdered anyone who interrupted them; he might have forced himself on Bet had she been unwilling. That she wasn't was the miracle. His hand slid up his shoulder to massage the stinging scratches. She had met him with a fury that nearly surpassed his own, and now he didn't know what to think or do or say. He was a breath away from plunging head-over-heels in love with her—a folly if ever there was one. No, he couldn't allow himself the luxury of loving Bet Valentine Calloway. He would always come off second best to the ghost of her husband, and his pride would not allow that.

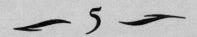

5

BET SIPPED HER coffee and stared past Jake's bent head.
The morning sun flickered through the fluttering leaves
of the chinaberry tree, striking patterns across the bay
window. The air was redolent with the aromas of a country breakfast, but Bet was scarcely aware of it, as she
was barely aware that her eyes followed the dance of the
sunlight. She couldn't seem to stop thinking about what
had happened in the hayloft, and it left her with a near
permanent blush. Two days, and Jake had not taken her
again. It was almost as though he were afraid to touch
her. Why else would he watch her with that curious
questioning gaze that slid away when she turned to him?

She still didn't understand what had happened, or how
it had happened, or, worst of all, why. Why? She needed
to know, but the crackling tension that sprang up between
them was completely outside her experience. It left her
feeling disjointed and out of control, a feeling she de-
tested. She wanted to respond to Jake. She wanted to
give him pleasure as he gave her pleasure, but she refused
to lose her heart. That belonged to John.

Bet sighed and put down her cup, rubbing one slender finger around the rim. It was an aberration. That was it. Something unique to time and place and circumstance. It wouldn't ever happen again.

Her spirits sank with the thought, and she shook her head irritably. How could she be so contrary? Of course she didn't want it to happen again! She wanted cool, calm control, not explosive passion without restraint or inhibition. She wanted peace and tranquillity, not wrenching, tearing desire.

Vagrant memory teased her with the smell of dust and hay, with the feel of sweat-slicked muscles and the taste of Jake's mouth. She wriggled about on her chair, her gaze clinging with something akin to desperation to a spark of light glancing off the rim of her cup. She would not look up at Jake!

Whether she looked or not, she knew his features as well or better than she did her own. The way his thick black hair sprang up from the widow's peak and waved away from his forehead. The tiny bump on his nose, as though it might have been broken at some time. The thick, wide-spaced eyebrows that arched slightly down his temples. His mouth, beautiful and so ready to smile. His eyes, a dark mystery of black with brownish flecks that seemed capable of reading her soul. His chest, molded by muscles and heavily peppered with curling hair.

How could she *not* know him? Jake Calloway was the man who had popped into her life and turned it topsy-turvy. He was the man who had taken a girl and made her a woman. A woman who knew now what it was to experience the ultimate ecstasy. A woman who knew what it was to desire and be desired. He had wakened her slumbering sensuality, and with it had come a heightened awareness of all the senses. Taste, smell, sight, feeling; she was alive as never before. There was only one dark cloud. Desire—without love.

With John it had been love without desire. A passive affection that healed the scars of her childhood. She had needed that—someone in this great empty world who saw in her something worthy of his love. It was as though John had unplugged a stopper in her heart and released the great gush of love she had hoarded for so long. She gave him everything she had and was rewarded with all she needed.

But somehow, now that she looked back on it, it seemed an empty, sterile kind of love. Was it only the contrast of Jake's vibrant love of life that made it seem so? Or, was it some lack in her? Had she been incapable of giving John what he needed? Was that why she could not banish the loneliness from his sad eyes? Would that lack in her leave her incapable of doing the same thing for Jake?

She stiffened, her finger slipping and setting the cup to rattling on the saucer. Why was she asking herself such a question? Jake didn't want that from her. *She* would not fill the emptiness in his life. The children she would give him would do that. She didn't even want to try! It would be too easy . . .

No! She wouldn't go through that again! She suffered agonies when John died! Any woman who loved Jake Calloway would be consumed. To love him and lose him would be unthinkable. It couldn't happen. It wouldn't happen. She wouldn't let it! She would be a good wife and a good mother, but she would keep a part of her heart inviolate.

She watched Jake mop up the last of the honey with a flaky, homemade biscuit and smiled to herself. He ate every meal as if it were going to be his last, and despite what his mother said, he lavished her with compliments. It must be the honeymoon. When they were a staid old married couple, he would be shoveling his meal, grunting, and lumbering off to work or to read the paper.

Jake caught her eye and grinned like a naughty little boy. Rocking back on the legs of his chair, he sighed. "Don't know what it is about marriage that makes a man so hungry."

Bet leaned forward. "Someone else doing the cooking."

"Guess so. Sure could use another cup of coffee," he wheedled.

Bet eyed the coffeemaker across the kitchen and skewered him with an arch look.

Jake leaned forward, threading his arm around salt and pepper shakers, a crumb-filled plate, and the jar of honey to capture her hand. One thumb rubbed slowly back and forth across her knuckles, sending a shiver of pleasure streaking up her arm. "I could have sworn you promised to love, honor, and . . . pamper."

"I would never be so foolish." She inched her tingling fingers from his loose grip and shoved her coffee cup toward him. "Mine's empty, too."

"Is this what they call a Mexican standoff?"

"Yup." She grinned.

"Tell you what. How's about I pamper you today, you pamper me tomorrow. Fair's fair, right?"

"Let's talk about that *after* you get my coffee."

"Woman—" he began with a teasing warning, but he broke off to listen. The ratcheting sound of a sick engine clattered above the soft drone of the air conditioner, and a look of consternation wrinkled across Jake's features. "Oh, hell! Bet, there's something I forgot to tell you. That's Rose. She's been coming to clean the house on Tuesdays and Fridays for years. Husband's got a bad back; hasn't worked since I've known him. She really needs this job, and I hope you won't mind keeping her on."

Bet gave him a troubled look. She loved this sprawling house and had been looking forward to keeping it herself: a damning admission for a modern woman. But, large as it was, there would be plenty of work for two. "I'll get fat and lazy," she warned with a smile.

Jake came around the table, dropping to one knee beside her. "You're an angel, and I'll take you any way I can get you." He brushed a light kiss across her lips.

"Heard you had a new missus!" The nasal squawk nearly knocked Bet off her chair and onto Jake's knee. "'Bout time. That's all I got to say. 'Bout time. Name's

Rosalinda Winston, Miz Calloway. But folks, they just call me Rose. You got a good man there. That's all I got to say. A good man."

Rose Winston sniffed through her long thin nose and tucked her nonexistent chin into her scrawny neck. A moment later her skinny rump was high in the air as she scrambled through the broom closet, withdrawing an apron, a mop, and a pail.

"You just get on with what you was at. Won't be bothering me none. I always start in the bathrooms. Best place to start, I always say. The bathrooms." She loped down the hall, leaving Bet gaping after her.

"You'll like Rose. She just takes a little getting used to. And 'that's all I got to say,'" Jake laughed, rising after bussing Bet on the cheek. "Gotta go. We're plowing the north forty today."

Bonnie had her usual playful meal—more in her hair than in her mouth—followed by a thorough bath. At loose ends, Bet took her out to the tiny swing chair Jake had put up in the pines the day before. She locked her into it and spread a quilt nearby, where she could reach out to give Bonnie a push when it slowed.

Bet read *Cinderella, Snow White,* Dr. Seuss, and was bored silly. Everything she wanted to do was in the house, but she didn't want to get in Rose's way. When Bonnie began nodding off, Bet took her in and put her down for a nap. Their things had all been neatly put away. There was nothing left to—

But there was! Her box of books. And she had seen an empty bookcase in one of the bedrooms. She hurried out to the garage and staggered back with the box, settling happily on the floor to arrange her treasures. She paused often, her hands rubbing across the covers, fingers tracing the gilt lettering before she opened them to flip through and read odd passages.

"Bet?"

"In here." Jake poked his head in and came to squat down beside her. "I thought you were plowing."

"Drive shaft broke. Man's coming out to fix it this afternoon." He lifted one of the books. *"Diary of a Refugee,* Frances Fearn. I'll be damned!" He lifted another book, this one bearing the crossed bars and stars of the Confederacy on a gray background. *"Recollections of a Rebel Reefer,* James Morris Morgan. I'll be damned!" he said in a sharp, awed voice. He began poking through the box, mumbling titles under his breath.

"Is something wrong?" Bet asked, utterly perplexed.

"No, something is very right." He pinned her with a curious stare until she began squirming. "I can't believe it! Have you seen my study?"

"Oh, no! I wouldn't..."

Jake dropped the book he was holding and frowned. "Bet, this is our house now. No room in it is closed to you. Come with me. There's something I want you to see."

He hurried down the hall with his long-legged stride, leaving Bet to run after him. Crossing the living room, he opened the door to his study and ushered her through.

"Look at the books on that wall."

She approached it cautiously, standing with her hands behind her back and her head cocked at an angle. Her eyes skipped from title to title, and her mouth dropped open. She whirled around, one hand fluttering at the wall of books. "These are all... all..."

"Louisiana history," he supplied. "I have a doctorate, Bet. That"—he waved toward the wall—"is my specialty."

"But why are you ranching? Why aren't you teaching?"

He grimaced. "Spare me yawning youth. I've yet to meet the college student who wasn't convinced he already knew it all, myself included. I prefer to write. I'm expanding my thesis into a full-fledged book about Shreveport in the Civil War."

"Oh, that's wonderful, Jake! Northern Louisiana has been criminally neglected by historians."

"True. Until recently, you'd think the only inhabited part of the state was New Orleans." He dusted off his

jeans and sank into the overstuffed leather sofa, patting
a place beside him. "Talk, woman. How did you get
interested enough to start collecting diaries and autobiog-
raphies from the Civil War?"

Bet ignored the sofa and curled up on the floor at his
feet. Jake smiled. He was learning about her. She never
sat in a chair if she could sit on the floor. She never
wore shoes if she could get away with going barefoot.
He eyed the pink pads of her toes with a lazy grin.

"That's dull," Bet said, folding her hands across his
knee and propping her chin on it. "I want to hear about
your book."

Jake's heavy eyebrows shot up in a teasing arch.
"That's dull. I want to hear about you." He tweaked her
freckled nose. "C'mon, tell Jake how a beautiful young
woman got interested in musty old history."

Bet pasted on a brittle smile and ignored the quivering
nausea that churned her stomach. "Is this going to be
another Mexican standoff?"

"Nope. Did Aunt Hester forget to mention that I'm a
stubborn cuss?" He rested his head on the back of the
sofa, stretched out his long legs, and laced his hands
across his middle. "I'm listening."

Bet practically felt her eyes dull to a muddy brown.
The hurt was always there, waiting to spring out and
grab her by the throat. She drew up her knees and wrapped
her arms around them, resting her cheek on one. "I—I
really don't want to talk about it, Jake. It isn't important."

He sat forward, one curled forefinger drawing her chin
up to his searching gaze. "Isn't it?" he asked quietly.

"Only to me."

"And me," he said firmly. "Everything that concerns
you or—or hurts you is important to me, Slugger. Tell
me," he urged in that quiet, compelling tone that was so
uniquely and irresistibly his.

Her head snapped up, the glitter of anger sparkling
through her blood. "I've never told anyone! Not even
John! Why should I tell you?"

The words hung in the air. Ugly words of anger and

rejection. Bet watched in horror as Jake recoiled, his expression of shock melting into hurt before his long lashes veiled his eyes. Why had she lashed out at him that way? she wondered wildly. He couldn't know he was asking her to shred her soul, to lay bare all of her own rejection and anger and pain.

"Jake," she began softly, but his voice sliced across hers.

"Sorry, Bet. I guess this is what they call invading your space. I, uh, I won't do it—"

"Don't go!" she cried as he began to rise. "Please, I do want to tell you about it!" And she did, she realized with a start of surprise. It was more than an effort to soothe his ruffled feelings. It was more than a desire to smooth the path of her marriage. She wanted to tell him. She needed to tell him because . . . because she knew that Jake would not offer the pity she had always avoided. He would listen, absorb it all, and care.

She watched him settle back and met his cautious liquid black gaze. "It's so much more than how I got interested in Louisiana history, Jake. It's everything that led up to it and followed. I've never been able to talk to anyone about it. Not—not about how I felt. Not even to Aunt Hester, and you know how determined she can be." She gave him a shaky smile.

Jake propped his elbows on his knees and caught her hand, pulling it to his lips. "You don't have to do this."

"I want to. I want you to understand, but I'm afraid . . ."

"I know," he said quietly.

"How?"

"Come up here," he urged, and Bet crawled onto his lap, sitting with her forehead resting against his cheek. She felt his shrug and his smile. "Do you think there's something we're missing, Slugger?"

His arms drew her closer, and she felt the sudden tension that drew across his chest, as though her answer was inordinately important to him. She leaned back and met his dark eyes. "I don't know," she faltered.

"We've got a good fifty years to figure it out. Let's

hope that will be enough," he said lightly, although there was a slight roughness in his voice. "Tell me about your mother, Bet. It starts there, doesn't it?"

Bet nodded. How did he always know what she thought and how she felt? She slid her head along his chest and stared out through the window, where blood-red blossoms climbed the rose trellis. She wanted to pour out all her heartache, all her loneliness, all her fears. But the words, when they came, were hesitant breaths of dry sound, devoid of emotion.

"She had red hair. That's all I remember about her. She left me at a gas station early one morning before it opened. It was cold. There was a note pinned to my sweater. It said my name was Elizabeth, I was five years old, and my birthday was July fourth. I remember the gas station man sitting me on his desk and buying me a Coke and riding in the police car. I kept asking if they were taking me to my mother."

The hushed silence that fell was a breathless respite. The comforting caress of Jake's hand moved over her back in the same circular motions she used to calm Bonnie. It made her want to laugh and cry at the same time, to raise her eyes to his in gratitude for his patience. She drew a shuddering breath.

"My first foster family, the Hunts, had no children of their own. They had waited too long to adopt, and I was their only foster child. They treated me like their own. After a while we all began to believe it was true. Mr. Hunt made wooden toys for me and took me to the park to play. We used to go to Lake Bisteneau for picnics in the summer. They were so proud when I learned how to swim. They told me over and over how smart I was and made me feel like the most special little girl in the whole world."

Her voice broke, and she stopped. Jake's hand rose to her shoulder and squeezed gently, and she rubbed her cheek against it.

"He was tall and skinny with a big Adam's apple, and she was short and fat and happy. They used to call each other Laurel and Hardy. Mrs. Hunt loved old things and old times. She would rock me by the hour, singing songs and telling stories that had passed down through her family. Her granddaddy fought in the Civil War. He was at Vicksburg, and she told me how they got so hungry during the siege that they had to eat their mules. I remember one day we made a bonfire in the backyard and wrapped biscuit dough around a stick to roast over the fire the way he said he'd had to do in the war. I was with them five years; then Mrs. Hunt got sick."

Bet shuddered, and Jake drew her closer. "I didn't understand why I had to leave. Mr. Hunt cried and Mrs. Hunt cried and I cried. Before the caseworker took me away, Mrs. Hunt gave me that copy of *Recollections of a Rebel Reefer*. It was her grandfather's, and she wanted me to have it to remember her by. I never saw either of them again."

Her voice caught on a sigh, and Jake's lips pressed lightly against her forehead. "What happened then, Bet?"

"Oh, not much. I was never in one home more than a year. Ask me anything about any school in Shreveport, and I can tell you. I went to them all."

Jake stared down at the bright cap of her hair. Gallant, he thought. It was an old-fashioned word. One her Mrs. Hunt would have approved. It seemed nothing short of incredible that Bet had survived such a childhood with her appealing vulnerability and soft, loving heart intact. He didn't think he would have been strong enough to overcome the bitterness she must have felt. She wouldn't want pity, but his heart ached with it. With that and something else, something that warmed him. Admiration and a strange sort of pride. Bet had shared her deepest hurt with him. No one else. Not her first husband, no one. Only him.

"Slugger," he said raggedly. Her small face turned up to him, her eyes huge with unshed tears. "Thank you," he whispered. Her face crumpled, and she burrowed into his chest. Her sobs shook them both, and Jake held her tightly, trying to swallow the lump in his throat.

"I hated it, Jake. I hated it!" she cried. "Always new faces and no one who cared!"

His hand cradled her head, and his lips moved against her brow. "It's over now. It's past. You're here with me. You're home, Slugger. Home."

She stirred and pulled back with a wide, wondering gaze. "Home?" she whispered through trembling lips.

"Will you get tired of this same old face?"

"Never!" she breathed. "I'm so happy here, Jake."

"Are you?" Suddenly her answer was the most important thing in Jake Calloway's world.

"Yes! I have Bonnie and your family—they're wonderful!—and . . . and you."

A distant third. Jake almost sighed aloud. It was better than nothing, but the idea that it might be an even more distant fourth, behind her beloved John, rankled no small amount. He made sure nothing of that thought showed on his face as he hooked one finger beneath Bet's chin and coaxed her head up.

"Imagine it: I got a wife and a collaborator all in one. Would you like to help me with my work?"

"Oh, yes! I'd love it! But—"

"But nothing. All you need is a love of the subject, and that you have." His lips brushed across hers. "I wonder what I ever did without you, Slugger."

It was there again. The tension that sparked excitement in Jake and roused Bet to apprehension. The heart-stopping cognizance of male and female, of mutual needs and mutual desires. The loss of self in a duality of interlocking passions.

Bet's hand rose and drifted to Jake's face. Her fingers touched his shadowed chin, delighting in the tiny prickles of his shaved skin. They inched up to his lips, ghosting across the upper and tracing the full lower. His tattered breath washed hot across her knuckles, and she shivered. She touched his nose, drew the arch of his brow with her thumb, and trailed her fingers along the single shallow crease on his forehead, absorbed by the sunburned darkness of his forehead and the creamy whiteness of her hands. Her palm wafted across his temple, and a single fingertip traced the shell of his ear. She heard the sharp intake of his breath. Her hand inched around his nape, her fingers toying with the short, close-cropped curls.

"Jake," she said, only her lips moving on a soundless sigh. Her drugged gaze clung to the lifeline of his eyes. A dim perception formed. A perception of patience quivering on the precipitous edge of forbearance, and she offered the gift of her lips. His mouth tasted her with a trembling eagerness, as though she were a fragile chimera that might vanish from his grasp.

It wasn't enough, that melding of lips. Bet moved, and Jake dragged his mouth from hers, his face tight with longing.

"Don't leave me now, Bet." The words were a ravished susurration.

"No, I won't," she soothed, and she moved again.

Understanding blossomed with a smile, and he stretched his legs out and lay back, sighing when she stretched out atop him. His skin was warm and tasted of salt, sweat, and the dust of the fields. The pulse at his throat pounded against her lips. Forefinger and thumb worked one button of his blue work shirt free, then another and another while his chest heaved and rippled beneath her. She spread the shirt wide, baring the heavily furred expanse of his chest. Her tongue flicked the hard brown pebble of one of his nipples, and she heard an inarticulate growl and felt the spasmodic clenching of his fingers at her waist.

The growl drew her head up, her expression hesitant. But she saw both acceptance and consent in the heavy-lidded, obsidian depths of his eyes and knew that with this man she was free to explore, to touch, to taste, to learn. There was no wrong, only the shared joy of giving and receiving pleasure. It was a new and arresting idea, and with it came a strange sense of power. It was with a child's curiosity that she tested the notion. Her hand skimmed lightly over his chest, and a delicate flurry of movement agitated the muscles she touched. She met his eyes once more, and her soft laugh was a seductive sound of triumph.

"Putty," Jake responded breathlessly. "What will you do with me?"

"This." She dipped her tongue into the shallow indentation at his throat. "And this." She nibbled the strong line of his jaw. "And this." She tugged at his lower lip, slicking her tongue over it, felt the rough texture of his palms sliding beneath her blouse and cupping her breasts, and learned how very tenuous the balance of power was.

He rolled her over until she sat on his updrawn knee, her head resting on his arm. His tongue was cool at the corner of her mouth, his hand hot on her sensitive breast. Her sharp, slicing breath drew a rumbling growl from him that held her own seductive sound of triumph.

"Tease me, will you?"

Their eyes met, twin flames blending to obliterate those meager nothings, power and triumph. Their ardent flame of desire met and matched and consumed in a tangle of arms and legs sliding to the eggshell-colored carpet.

A moted beam of sunlight brightened the small hand with arched fingers that rushed feverishly across the undulating contours of his bare brown back. It glinted off the zipper of his discarded jeans and faded the soft pink of her lacy briefs that draped like a weary umbrella across the pencil jar atop the desk. It glanced off Jake's hair with a sheen of blue and turned Bet's bronze hair to glowing red embers. It molded the erotic dance of love in light and shadow.

Bet was lost to reason and thought. She was one throbbing nerve stretching, stretching toward the looming peak of fulfillment. It rushed toward her, arriving with a blinding flash and an explosion of exquisite pain. She floated like a drifting leaf to the golden valley of bliss, with Jake's lips nuzzling the tender curve of her neck on shredded whispers of sound.

She blinked and started violently, her fingers digging

into Jake's sides. He jerked up and stared down at her with wide eyes. Together they listened to the roaring of the vacuum cleaner in the living room and the nasal sharpness of Rose Winston's vigorous hymn-singing.

Bet saw the twitching begin at the corners of Jake's mouth. "Don't you dare laugh!" she hissed. "This isn't funny!"

"It's no tragedy either." He grinned. "You're my wife. What could be more natural—"

"Natural!" Bet cried in an agony of embarrassment. "There's nothing natural about this! We're no better than—"

"Don't say it!" His expression was so cold and forbidding it gave Bet a chill of fear. "Don't even think it! You are my wife! I won't have you bringing any medieval ideas about right and wrong to my bed or anywhere else we might make love. Can you honestly say that anything that feels this right is wrong?"

It was her own question echoed back to her in a hard, angry voice. Could she? Honestly? No.

"Bet," Jake whispered in a voice threaded with tenderness, "can't you feel what's happening?"

It was impossible to break the gentle tether of his gaze. Her lips moved. "No."

She watched the tender light in his eyes wink out as though a candlewick had been pinched between ruthless fingers. He nodded and rolled away and stood, holding out an impersonal hand to help her rise. They dressed in silence with the roar of the vacuum cleaner just beyond the door. Bet watched him go, his back rigid and unrelenting, and fought back the painful ache of tears pressing against her throat.

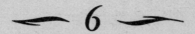

6

THE WEEK PASSED with an undercurrent of strain. It was to be expected, Bet assured herself. After all, they were strangers. The surface might appear familiar, but beneath lay the uncharted terrain of two disparate personalities. Whether they would rub each other raw or knit together into one complementary whole, only time would tell.

The strain was nothing she could define. She just knew that something had altered in their relationship. It was maddeningly subtle and elusive. She would have said she detected a reticence in Jake, but how could that be when he laughed with her, teased Rose unmercifully, and played with Bonnie? At night he turned to her with a wholesome relish that banished her last niggling doubts about right and wrong.

He was her husband. She had committed herself to him for better or worse, only there seemed to be no worse. With each day that passed, she found more in him to admire and respect. It was increasingly easy to accept his embraces, to look forward to them and match her mood to his. Sometimes he swept her up in a zestful frolic that kept her giggling until passion caught her with breathtaking haste. Sometimes he was achingly tender, frustratingly slow, carrying her inch by languid inch into a starry night of rapture.

Yet there was a difference. As if he, too, was holding a part of himself back. As if he, too, was haunted by that soft question threaded with tenderness: "Bet, can't you feel what's happening?"

She might deny it to him, but she couldn't deny it to herself. There was something beyond the powerful sexual attraction that electrified them in unguarded moments. It winked on and off like the phosphorescent green flash of the lightning bugs that flitted through the dusky summer evenings. But each time it came, it lasted longer and left her with a stronger feeling of well-being. It happened often when their eyes met over Bonnie's crib at night: a tiny suspension of time, the submersion of their two separate selves into one whole bound together by the mutual desire to protect her daughter in a cocoon of love. It happened at meals when their eyes met and fused with a smile. It happened when they leaned over Jake's manuscript, sharing his knowledge and her interest.

Like the waves climbing the seashore, the contentment washed over Bet and then succumbed to the sucking tide of strain. Was Jake closing a door to his inner self? Was he shutting her out? It was a dog-in-the-manger attitude that she deplored, but she found herself wanting more from Jake than she was willing to give. Her penitent conscience twinged painfully and began to plague her with nightmares of abandonment and loss.

"Bet! Bet, wake up!"

She pried her sticky eyelids open. "Wha...what?"

Jake leaned over her, his dark face mellowed with concern as he smoothed the tangle of bronze waves from her forehead. "You were having a bad dream."

She bit her lip and rolled her head on the pillow,

evading his hand. The dream hovered like a word on the tip of the tongue, a tantalizing presence without overt form.

"Want to tell me about it?"

The question rumbled with compassion, but Bet shook her head, swallowing hard.

"Want to think about something else?"

She stared through the window and nodded.

"Good!"

The gusty sound edged in excitement drew her eyes to him. His black hair stood up in tufts about his head, and he was grinning like a mischievous little boy with a delicious secret. The dregs of the nightmare tiptoed into oblivion, and Bet found her smile taking life in her heart before it reached her lips.

"Do you know what day this is?"

She thought for a moment. "Saturday."

"That, too."

He waited expectantly while Bet scurried fruitlessly for an answer. "Sorry, I'm a little fuzzy for twenty questions."

"Today," he drawled, waggling his brows, "is our one-week anniversary, and I have a surprise for you. So get up and get dressed, lazybones. Jeans, not shorts. Mom's promised to keep Bonnie for us."

And that was that. Not a single question would he answer. Bet showered while he shaved and hummed to the mirror. Jake fed Bonnie while she fixed breakfast and burned with curiosity. He washed the dishes while she bathed Bonnie and shouted her guesses down the hall. For her pains she received the rattling of pots and pans and muffled laughter. By the time they left the house, Bet was in a state of feverish anticipation—which, she suspected, was exactly how he wanted her.

She gave Bonnie a last kiss before she was pulled down the back steps of the main Calloway house. "Where are we going?"

Jake draped an arm across her shoulders and snuggled

her into the curve of his body. "You'll see."

Bet puckered her lips in an exaggerated pout, slued a glance to gauge its effect, and found his obnoxiously smug grin slipping a notch wider.

"You'll see" was all he had to say.

They strolled at a leisurely pace. The chickens squawked and strutted, darting their beaks at unseen tidbits hiding in the grass. The garden was a lush green, the plants heavy with brilliant red tomatoes, dark purple eggplants, and clusters of peas and beans. The narrow footpath, worn to dirt, branched off toward the stables, and Jake led her along it, whistling a monotonous scale that made her long to kick him in the shins.

They reached the paddock where a single horse munched on a pile of hay. Jake removed his arm from her shoulder, folded his forearms along the top rail, and rested his chin on his elbow. "Happy Anniversary, Bet." He smiled.

Her tawny eyes widened with uncertainty. A horse! If she had been given a thousand guesses, she would never have been right. A horse!

"She's yours," Jake said as the mare nudged his shoulder with her muzzle and rolled curious velvety brown eyes at Bet.

"Mine?" Bet quavered while the idea that she was to have her very own horse took root with a vengeance. What did she know about horses? The only one she had ever mounted had been a stick horse that she rode in the red and yellow felt cowgirl suit Santa put under her tree at the Hunts' one year. But she was delighted. Her very own horse! She could ride with Jake and take his lunch out to the fields when he was working.

Jake straightened, nervously shifting his weight from one foot while he propped the other on the lower rail and began to rub the horse's nose. "She's a strawberry roan." He rubbed his thumb against the nap of her hide. "See the mixture of chestnut and white hair? That's what gives her this color. The white strip from forelock to muzzle is called a blaze. She's got full stockings," he babbled uneasily. "See the white from just above her knees to her hooves? She's a good sound mare, Bet. And gentle. I knew she'd be perfect for you the first time I saw her."

"She—she's beautiful."

"Yes, she is that."

Bet thrust her hands behind her, like a child facing a piece of candy she dared not touch. "What's her name?"

"Daisy Mae," Jake said with a disgusted grimace. "I hope you'll change it."

"I think . . . I think . . . Rhapsody?"

"Rhapsody. I like that." Jake moved restlessly. "I, uh, I thought you might like to have a horse. We ride on the place a lot, and I hope, uh, well, it would be nice if you knew something about the ranch and the cattle."

Bet watched him rub his hand along the back of his neck and heard the hesitancy in his voice. He was uncertain about her reception of his gift! She knew she should set his mind at ease at once, but couldn't resist the urge to tease him.

She gave him a look of wide-eyed innocence. "I'm not completely ignorant, Jake," she said with a touch of asperity. "I know that a Brahman has a hump on its back and a Hereford is red with a white face."

His face went so blank Bet found it impossible to maintain her innocent look. A giggle erupted, and she flung out her arms, launching herself at him much the way his nephew Archie was fond of doing. She hooked her ankles behind his narrow hips and hugged him tightly, her laughter tripping up the scale as he whirled her around and around, stirring up a cloud of dust as his own relieved laughter blended with hers.

"God, Bet! I thought I'd put my foot in it! You *do* like her, don't you?"

She leaned back, her fingers laced at his nape. "I love her! She's the best present anybody ever gave me. But . . . but, Jake, I've never been on a horse in my life! What if I can't ride?"

"With the best teacher in the parish? Don't worry, I'll have you in championship form in no time. You'll think you were born in the saddle."

"I don't know," she said doubtfully.

"I do. Trust me, Slugger."

"Always," she said softly. "You've been so good to me, Jake."

"It's..." He cleared the husky rasp from his throat. "It's easy to be good to you, Bet." His head dipped, and their lips met in a gentle quest that searched and deepened.

"Hell, Jake! You ain't got her on that horse yet?"

Pete's gravelly voice punctured their engrossed communings with an effect similar to that of a pin in a balloon.

Bet's locked ankles sprang apart. Jake's head jerked up. Bet's legs slid along him until she came to rest leaning lightly against him while his arm shielded her. She looked up and found him glaring at his brother over her head.

"Jake," she said in quiet warning.

Pete was oblivious to the look that passed between them. He laughed and climbed atop the fence. Cocking his hat at an angle on his rusty brown hair, he winked and grinned at Bet. "Thought he might need some help with your first lesson. Since I taught him everything he knows, I expect you'd like advice from a *real* expert."

"And who taught you both?" Jake's father called out as he came up the path, trailed by the quieter Burt. "Well, Bet, what do you think of her? Jake almost fell off his seat at the auction barn when they trotted her into the ring. No telling what he would have ended up paying if it hadn't been a quiet day."

Bet pressed her cheek to Jake's chest and raised a soft, loving gaze. "Thank you."

His chest swelled, and he began to speak, but his father interrupted. "You'll have to get her used to your voice and the feel of your hands. Come over here and talk to her."

"Here." Jake dug chunks of carrots from his pocket and dropped them into Bet's hand. "Place a piece in your palm and stretch your fingers out flat when you feed her."

It was all she could do to keep still while Rhapsody sniffed at the carrot. Bet was convinced she was going to lose a finger or two. But when Rhapsody lipped it up with a deft motion, Bet's confidence soared. Soon, under her father-in-law's tutelage, she was running her hands across the rippling muscles of the mare's shoulders, scratching her blaze, and burying her face in the flowing mane with a soft gurgle of happy laughter.

She was ready to jump on and ride, but Pete dragged out the tack, taking her step by step through the intricate process of putting on the bridle and bit, positioning the blanket, and setting the saddle in place. When the girth was tightened to his satisfaction, he laced his fingers and bent over.

"Take the pommel—"

"Whoa, there!" Jake came off the fence. "I'll take over from here. Wouldn't want you to have all the fun."

"Bet"—Pete grinned—"you sure you don't want the *real* expert?"

"Whooey! Listen to him!" Jake hooted. "She's got the real expert! Find yourself a perch on that fence and watch a master at work." Jake laced his fingers together. "Hold the pommel and put your foot in here. I'll give you a boost."

Bet vaulted into the saddle, squirmed around, and beamed down at Jake. "This feels wonderful!"

"You won't be staying on long if you don't learn how to sit properly." One dark hand ran down her leg to position thigh and knee and foot. He was all impersonal instructor, but the firm stroking of his palm and the gentle pressure of his fingers sent tremors undulating along Bet's nerves.

"We'll have to get you some boots. These tennis shoes won't do." His hand skimmed up her shins to recheck the positioning of her knee. "You need to grip firmly." His fingers slipped between her thigh and the saddle flap, and her breath fluttered through parted lips. "Press, don't squeeze. Just a firm grip. Good, that's right."

Bet's blush burned against the heat of the day. Her wide gaze fled any meeting with his eyes, drifting upward to watch the chittering flight of a quartet of sparrows. His hand slid up her thigh, the touch lighter, more caressing than impersonally firm, and her heart began a trip-hammer beat. She flinched slightly when one hand splayed across her abdomen and the other pressed against the base of her spine.

"Relax."

Every muscle rebelled. Despite any command to the contrary her spine stayed rigid and ramrod straight. The heel of his hand rode the shallow valley of her back, up and down in slow movements that were anything but soothing. Her stomach tied itself in a knot and looped itself into a quivering bow. She hazarded a glance and found his lips promising laughter and his eyes glinting with amusement.

"You..." She leaned down to hiss. "You're doing this on purpose!"

"Yup." The promised smile sprang to life, bright and sunny, and the pale squint lines at the corners of his eyes crinkled. "Devil made me do it," he confided.

"Did he?" she asked dryly, one bronze eyebrow arching high. She reached out, running her fingers along the rim of his Stetson before pinching the brim between forefinger and thumb. The hat sailed away, and her fingers threaded through his hair, cupping the back of his head and sliding down his nape as she bent lower. Her lips pressed against the corner of his mouth and moved flirtatiously across his. She felt the convulsion of his fingers at her waist, and she raised her head, meeting his burning gaze with a winsome smile.

"You kick that old devil in the seat of the pants," she whispered in her best exaggerated drawl, "and pay attention to what you're doing."

"Hell, woman!" Jake croaked and cleared the frog from his throat.

A round of applause, shrill whistling, and loud cheering propelled Jake around. Bet gave her laughing father-in-law a jaunty salute and relaxed in the saddle, watching with a smile as Jake turned back to her.

"Tonight," he mouthed in a silent threat that sent joy bubbling through her veins with the heady effervescence of champagne.

Joy. It was a new word in Bet Calloway's vocabulary. One whose every thrilling nuance she savored as the summer waxed hot and dusty beneath the broiling southern sun. Her nights were a succession of soft, sweet, glorious episodes of lovemaking. Her days began at dawn with the cock's crow, just as Jake had promised. After a few mornings of dragging reluctantly from the bed, she found she enjoyed the sight of the sun rising over the ragged skyline while she ran water into the coffeepot and listened to Jake singing in the shower. While she cooked breakfast, Jake tumbled about on the living room rug with Bonnie until it was time to put her in her carrier and bring her to the table. There he would ruffle her strawberry curls and try to teach her to say *Daddy*.

Bet learned to harvest vegetables from the huge communal garden and spent long mornings with Mother Calloway and her sisters-in-law, Terry and Marlene, canning and preserving in the huge old farmhouse kitchen. Plump, giggling Terry kept them laughing, but it was the more serious Marlene who did the most work.

Bet never tired of grooming Rhapsody, and she spent a part of every day in the stable feeding her mare carrots and sugar cubes. Within a month she was riding like a somewhat awkward centaur and loving every minute of her gallops with Jake and his brothers or father.

On Saturdays there was a trip to the old-time country store run by Mom and Pop Jensen. The bare wooden floors creaked with every step, and the smooth wooden counter was lined with glass jars of Jawbreakers, Red Hots, licorice sticks, and candy canes. It was an Ali Baba's cave filled with unusual treasures and loosely guarded by the elderly Jensens, who much preferred to pull up an old wooden rocker with a split-oak seat and exchange community gossip than to make a sale. Bet loved poking in the dusty corners and finding old-fashioned nutcrackers, galvanized milk pails with long rubber nipples for feeding calves, crockery butter churns, and bowls of all shapes and sizes.

Her greatest find in the country store settled a question that had been perplexing her. Tucked in a corner of a dusty glass display case was a tall pile of plaid handkerchiefs in outlandish colors. Now she knew where Archie got his handkerchiefs!

On Sundays there was a quiet service in the country church down the road, then a huge meal with Jake's parents, followed by a lazy afternoon during which, more often than not, Bonnie fell asleep on Jake's chest and Bet snoozed in the curve of his arm.

June waned in a blistering heat. Leaves hung limp in the still air, and flowers drooped on their dusty stems. Bet began to notice that Jake stopped singing in the shower. A frown wrinkled his brow with increasing frequency, and his dark liquid eyes watched her with something very near accusation. A tremor quaked through her happy life. Although she scoured her mind for something she might have done, she could think of nothing.

Her hesitant attempts to question him met with no success. When he marched out in an ill temper one hot morning, she decided to take action. First she would ply him with a special noontime meal. Then, by hook or by crook, she would get him to talk.

Everything worked for her. Rose was going to be late that day, not arriving until two. Marlene came for Bonnie, and Bet left the house while the dew was still damp on the grass. Pail in hand, she tromped through waist-high weeds to find the plump, luscious blackberries she had seen on one of her rides with Jake. The smooth brown surface of the pond reflected the drifting clouds as she angled alongside it, moving off toward the treeless, weed-choked area dotted with tall sprawling clumps of blackberry vines. One by one the fat, purplish-black berries thumped into the bottom of the pail, covering it and climbing the sides. Sweat trickled between her breasts and briers tore at her hands, but Bet hummed cheerfully. If the way to a man's thoughts was through his stomach, she would know what was troubling him before the day was done.

Her pail brimming, she hurried back to the house to whip up a cobbler, put on dinner, and dash down the hall to shower before Jake came in from plowing.

Jake drove the tractor under the shade of the sweet gum tree, climbed off, and tugged at his work gloves. His eyes lifted to the open loft door, and his breath quickened. "Dammit," he muttered, slamming his gloves down on the metal tractor seat. What in the name of hell was wrong with him? He took off his battered straw hat and raked his dusty forearm across his sweating brow. He should be satisfied. He had everything a man could ask for, didn't he?

Hell, yes! His house was spotless. His meals were perfect. His clothes were always fresh. He not only had a wife, he had a collaborator. He didn't have to struggle with that pesky typewriter. The letter-perfect manuscript was neatly aligned in a manila folder, each day's scrawled pages ready for his inspection the next morning. If he needed an obscure reference point, it was Bet who spent hours leafing through books to find it for him. More often, to his amazement, she already knew where it was. She was an angel, Bet Valentine Calloway!

Could any man ask for more in a wife than that marvel of energy, patience, and thoughtfulness? he asked himself sourly as he strode down the rutted road, kicking at clods of dirt. Well, could he? He was still wondering when he stomped through his door and stopped short.

The flowery essence of Bet's favorite perfume blended with the mouth-watering aroma of rump roast studded with garlic and onion. Jake looked into the living room, stared down the hall, and scoured the kitchen. No one.

So why was Bet all dressed up and looking as cool and delicious as a bowl of sherbet?

"Are we expecting company?" he growled.

A slice of bread scuttled across the counter, the knife clattered to the floor, and Bet whirled around. "Jake! I didn't hear you come in! Company?" She smoothed her frosty yellow wraparound skirt with a self-conscious gesture and gave him a soft smile. "I see I'll have to dress up just for you more often."

His mood lightened at that admission, and a reluctant smile tugged at his lips. "I don't know. I kind of like your shorts—and the legs that go with them."

Her cheeks pinkened, and Jake leaned against the counter, arms folded across his chest as he watched her retrieve the knife.

"Hungry?" she asked.

"Starving."

That gravelly insinuation brought her head up to meet his warming gaze. "Jake . . ."

He stalked across the kitchen with a purposeful stride, the light of playful lechery sparkling in his eyes. "Starving," he repeated with a breathless catch that could not leave the least doubt as to which of his appetites was paining him.

His lips smothered Bet's startled "Oh!" One arm pressed her to him while the dark fingers of his opposite hand slid into her short, waving hair. Her cool hand touched his nape, but the sensation was more like the hot kiss of a branding iron. His mouth moved over hers with tempting, teasing persuasion, and the scalding heat of desire spread through his belly.

"God, woman! You make me feel like I'm eighteen again. How long has it been since last night?"

Her heavy-lidded sultry look set his heart to thumping, and the nibbling kiss pressed to his throat sent a chill scrabbling down his backbone. "Too long," she murmured.

His triumphant laugh wavered on a growl, and he reached down to sweep her into his arms. He took a step toward the hall, his mouth locked on hers, and the door burst open, crashing against the wall.

"Aunt Bet, you got cookies?" a piping voice asked.

Jake turned around to meet the astonished stare of his nephew, Archie.

"Is Aunt Bet hurt?"

"No, she's not hurt," Jake eked out between clenched teeth.

"Why you holding her like that?" came the curious question Jake would have expected if he hadn't been so consumed by frustration that he was incapable of anticipating anything.

He rolled his eyes to the ceiling, praying for patience. It wouldn't do to tell his nephew that he was planning to ravish his willing wife. It wouldn't do at all. Black orbs rolled down and were lost in the shadows of his narrowed lashes.

"Do you know how to knock, young man?"

"Y-yes, sir, but I never knock—"

"You will from now on, and you will wait until someone opens the door. Is that clear?"

"Y-yes, sir," Archie answered with an owlish stare.

"Jake, don't be so hard on him," Bet whispered in his ear as she slid from his arms.

He let her go. Propping his hips against the counter edge, he folded his arms across his chest and watched them both with a jaundiced glare. A suspicious sparkle turned Bet's tawny eyes a bright gold, and she seemed to have some trouble controlling the twitching corners of her mouth. She wouldn't dare, Jake thought with a frown.

Archie got his cookies and was sent off with a kiss and a few murmured words from his adored Aunt Bet, who leaned against the door with shaking shoulders. When she turned at last, her shimmering gaze met Jake's offended one, and she burst into a cascade of giggles.

He could believe neither his eyes nor his ears. It wasn't possible that she could find this funny! His stiff arms peeled away from his chest, and his fingers clenched like

vises around the cabinet ledge on either side of him as
he watched her run across the kitchen with her arms
outstretched and her merry laughter bubbling like a wa-
terfall. Her arms slipped around his waist, her freckled
nose bumped into his unyielding chest, and she raised
her bright golden gaze to his face.

Her laughter choked off, and she eased her arms from
him, backing away. "I'm sorry," she squeaked; then she
clapped her hand over her mouth to smother another
eruption of giggles.

"There is nothing funny about it." Every word dropped
like a ten-ton weight.

She sucked in a deep breath and lowered her brimming
eyes. "Of course not," she soothed.

"Don't patronize me, Bet!" he snapped.

"What's wrong, Jake?" She stepped close, her hands
resting along his ribs. "You haven't been yourself in
days."

He stared down at her, his eyes drifting lightly across
her face. How could he tell her what was wrong with
him when he didn't know himself? "I'm going to take
a shower," he said gruffly, dodging her and starting down
the hall.

"I'll have your dinner ready when you get out."

He knew he should have answered, but he didn't. He
was afraid he would let out a howl of frustration if he
dared open his mouth. In their room he paused, staring
at the bed, then stripped off his clothes and hopped into
the steaming shower. She shouldn't encourage the kids
to run in and out all day, he fumed silently. If she wouldn't
keep the cookie jar full, his house wouldn't be worse
than an airport terminal. Hell, he couldn't come in during
the day without tripping over Terry or Marlene. And
when he wanted to have a late, lazy morning, two abed,
Bet always had something planned with his mother. He
couldn't even take her riding without Pete or Burt or Dad
coming along! And she wondered what was wrong with
him! He couldn't get five minutes alone with his own
wife! That was what was . . .

Jake's jaw dropped open. He was jealous of his own family! And was that a real chuckle! *He* was the one with the brilliant idea of using his family to woo Bet into marriage. He'd realized it was her weak spot, and he'd used it. So why was he complaining because it worked even better than he'd expected?

She was happy. Bonnie was happy. His family loved them both. He was . . .

He'd be a fool not to be happy! Bet was the perfect wife! He couldn't ask for more than she had given. Could he? No. Did he want to? Yes. Hell!

He stepped from the shower, snatched up a towel, and rubbed himself vigorously. If he couldn't ask any more of her, he could . . .

A honeymoon! The thought struck with the staggering force of lightning. A gleeful smile wound across his face. Perfect! He'd get her away for a few days. Wine her. Dine her. And, best of all, have her all to himself! He could hardly wait to get dressed and tell her.

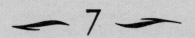

7

MEN, BET THOUGHT with fond disgust as she finished slicing the warm loaf of bread. They had absolutely no sense of humor when it came to...

She stopped to laugh softly to herself. She would never forget Jake's expression of acute frustration! Whatever *he* thought, *she* thought it was funny. Poor Archie; his eyes had been as big as saucers. She arranged the bread on the plate, sliced the roast, filled the gravy boat, and dished up a crockery bowl of fluffy, steaming rice. After carrying the last dish to the table, she peeked into the oven to check on the cobbler. Satisfied that all was ready, she debated whether to call Jake.

It wasn't necessary. A broom handle waved to and fro in the hall door. On its end fluttered a gaudy Archie handkerchief. "Truce! Truce!" Jake called out.

Bet choked back a gurgle of laughter and took her life in her hands. "Are you over your, um, your snit?"

The tip of the broom dropped to the floor in a puddle of black and yellow plaid. Jake appeared, hands on hips.

"Snit? Is that what you call it?" His tone was outraged, but his face was alight with suppressed laughter. "There I was, all ready to let you ravish me"—his eyebrows wagged—"as you were so willing to do, and—"

"Funny," Bet drawled, slanting him a wicked look, "that isn't how *I* remember it. As *I* remember it, *you* were the one—"

"Tsk, tsk, tsk." Jake shook his head. "I think we're going to have to do something about that faulty memory of yours."

The broom thudded to the floor, and Jake began rounding the bar. His hair was damp from the shower, one lock falling across his freshly scrubbed forehead. His western plaid shirt was unbuttoned, revealing a swirling thatch of black hair that narrowed and dipped into the waistband of the faded jeans that snugged across his hips. He was gloriously healthy, vitally alive, and Bet felt a keen bit of regret that Archie had interrupted them. Unfortunately Rose was due at any time. She spread her fingers across Jake's chest to hold him off. "Hungry?"

"Starving," he insinuated in a basso profundo.

"I think this is where I came in," she said breathlessly, her hands betraying her intentions by treacherously gliding to the crest of his shoulders. She caught a glimpse of his dark eyes, seared clean of laughter, before his lips descended on hers. They moved over her mouth with a rough urgency that melted her last feeble resistance. She arched against him and felt the hard bulge of his manhood and heard the harsh rasping intake of his breath.

"Bet." His mouth slid along her cheek and nibbled at the lobe of her ear. "Bet, I—" Suddenly his head snapped up, and he stilled to listen.

Bet raised a heavy-lidded gaze to his face. "What—"

Then she heard it, too. The ratcheting sound of a sick engine. Rose! Her head dropped to his chest, and her fingers dug into his arms. "Oh, no!"

Jake's chest began to shake. "I should have known it was too good to last. We'll never have any privacy around here," he chuckled in her ear. "Why don't we take a trip? Just for a few days." Bet raised her head. "We can go anywhere you want. We can take Bonnie or leave her here with Mom and Dad. What do you say? Just us. Alone. No interruptions. A belated honeymoon?"

"I—I'd like that." It was a massive understatement. She'd love it! The idea that Jake really wanted to spend time alone with her filled Bet with an elation whose roots she would not examine too closely.

The door swung open, and Rose trotted across the threshold. "Evenin', ya'll," she squawked. "Got through early, so I come on." She hung her purse on a hook beside the door. A moment later her skinny rump was high in the air as she began scrambling through the broom closet. "You just get on with what you was at," she said as she loped toward the hall. "Won't be bothering me none. I always start in the bathrooms. Best place to start, I always say. The bathrooms."

As she vanished, Jake nuzzled Bet's neck. "Should we 'get on with what we was at'?"

Bet sighed wistfully. "Your dinner's getting cold."

"If it does, it'll be the only thing that's cold around here," he grumbled.

"Oh, no." Bet squirmed out of his arms and led him to the table. "Eat!"

Jake plowed through his meal while Bet picked at hers and tried to ignore the irritating frustration of being interrupted a second time. Somehow her humor had failed her.

"You look a thousand miles away," Jake said lazily as he shoved his empty plate aside.

"Oh, not so far," she twinkled ruefully. "I was just telling myself how sorry I am for laughing at you earlier."

"Ah." He reached out to catch her hand.

Bet snatched it away with a laugh. "Are you ready for dessert?" His brows climbed suggestively. "Not that kind! I've made you a special surprise."

The cobbler was done to perfection, and Bet set it directly in front of Jake with a flourish. The crisply browned latticework crust sparkled with crystals of sugar.

Sauce and berries bubbled, staining the edges of the crust a reddish-purple. It smelled like heaven and looked scrumptious.

Bet's bright smile was tinged with pride. Aglow with a sense of accomplishment, she looked from her special dessert to Jake's face. As she watched, the color drained from his cheeks and beads of sweat popped out and shimmered across his forehead. His eyes were riveted to the cobbler, wide and brilliant with horror. Her smile wavered, a puzzled frown growing.

"Black . . . blackberry . . . cobbler." The words wrenched from him on guttural grunts of loathing. "Where . . . where did you get the . . . the berries?" he asked in a hoarse, hollow voice, his eyes still riveted to the sparkling crust.

Bet's hands clenched around the plump potholders, drawing them to her chest like a shield. What was happening? What had she done wrong? "I—I picked them," she faltered on a thinning note of dismay.

"Where?"

"Near the pond."

His head snapped up, his eyes latching onto hers with terrifying intensity. She saw his chest heaving, the constricted muscles moving like ropes beneath the heavy furring of hair. His nostrils flared wide to struggle for air. Abruptly his lips drew back over his teeth in a snarl, and he vaulted from his chair.

The chair hit the floor with a crash, and Bet fell back a step, frightened by the fury that worked in Jake's face with pumping veins and writhing muscles. This was a man she didn't know and didn't want to know. A dark, mystifying side of him that made her quake with fear. She wanted to break all contact with the feverish, almost maniacal intensity of his burning eyes, but she found herself caught like a craven rabbit in a glare of light. She chewed on her quivering lower lip, her feet rooted to the floor as he reached for her with hard, angry hands that closed around her arms with a viselike grip. She was jerked close to his chest, her eyes still locked with his.

"Dammit!" he roared. "You will never bring blackberries into this house again! You will never pick them again! You will never—never—go to the pond alone again! Is that clear?"

"Jake," she quailed, blinking back tears of shock and terror, "you—you're hurting me."

His face twisted, and his fingers peeled away from her arms. He stepped back and raked his trembling hands through his hair. The rage died, leaving Jake's eyes dazed and wary, shiny disks of black that raced across her features as though they were alien to him. He reached out to touch her. Bet flinched, fearing another bruising grip, but his hands were gentle as they coasted along her shoulders and cupped her cheeks.

"Bet," he said softly, "you could have . . ."

A frown cleft a crease between his eyebrows. A frown that grew blacker the longer his eyes probed hers with a sharp-edged question. Suddenly he swiveled around. Bright black eyes dropped to the steaming cobbler. His dark hand swept down, lifted it, and tossed it through the bay window with a growl of rage.

It was a nightmare, with every sound and movement distinctly defined. Jake's dark fingers wrapping around the handle of the small Corningware pot. His elbow flexing and stretching as though propelled by his discordant growl. Tiny rays of sunlight streaking from the crystals of sugar. Droplets of berries and sauce splattering the table, floor, and window with soft plopping sounds. It seemed to Bet she could even see the point of contact, the edge of the bowl striking the windowpane, the webbing of spreading cracks, the brittle explosion of shattering glass.

Her heart throbbed in her throat as she watched one last sliver begin to tremble and tumble outside, its knifelike edges colored by sunlight. Slowly her wide, petrified gaze moved to Jake. Dear God, what would he do next?

His eyes met hers and held them. Bet shivered violently. She could neither look away nor read the confusing array of emotions that flickered in his eyes like an old movie. His frown deepened, and one hand curled into a tight fist that wakened Bet's every nerve with the scald of acid fear. It was unwarranted. Without explanation or apology, Jake rushed out of the house, slamming the door behind him.

Bet gripped the back of a chair, slowly easing herself into the seat as though she would crumble if she weren't careful. She stared at the single shattered pane in the bay window with numb astonishment, her thoughts traveling the rutted path of a broken record, looping back to begin again. *Jake burned his hand. The pot was too hot. He burned his hand.* Like a victim of shell shock, she clung to that single undeniable fact. *Jake burned his hand.*

"Miz Calloway!" Rose shook Bet's shoulder. "Miz Calloway! You all right?"

"I—I think so." *Jake burned his hand.*

"What happened?"

"I don't know." *The pot was too hot. Jake burned his hand.*

"Lord a'mercy!" Rose shrieked. "What happened to that window?"

Bet propped her elbow on the table and scrubbed at the ache across her forehead. "Jake . . ." His name faded to nothing, and she swallowed hard. "Jake threw the cobbler through it."

"He threw—" Rose jerked like a puppet controlled by a novice puppeteer. Her head jutted forward on the sticklike stem of her neck, and her long nose sniffed the air suspiciously. "Blackberry! Lord a'mercy! You done made that man a blackberry cobbler!" She wrung her rough, red hands. "Didn't nobody tell you?"

"Tell me what?" Bet asked dully. *Jake burned his hand.*

"Coffee!" Rose screeched in a perfect non sequitur. "There ain't nothing like a good cup of coffee to take a body's mind off her troubles. That's what I always say. Coffee!"

Jake burned . . . Bet looked up. "Rose, tell me what?"

Rose's pointed elbows flapped at her sides. "Miz Calloway"—her homely face screwed up in a pained expression—"somebody should have told you."

"Told me what!" Bet's voice climbed on a sharp edge of exasperation.

"It ain't my place..."

"Somebody has to tell me! Please." Bet stood and caught Rose's arm, leading her to a chair and pressing her into it. "Just tell me."

"Well, Mister Jake was always partial to blackberries. His mama used to laugh that she could roast them to coals and he'd still think they was good. But... but..."

"Go on," Bet prompted.

"Since Miz Tricia died, he can't stand the sight of one."

A cold chill of premonition washed over Bet. "I don't understand."

"Miz Tricia was back at the pond picking berries for a cobbler when that snake bit her," Rose whispered. "After the funeral Mister Jake come back here and burned off that whole field. He was plumb wild with grieving, he was. Got down as skinny as a rail and forgot how to smile. And you know that ain't Mister Jake! He was always one for funning. I always say there ain't nobody likes his little jokes better than Mister Jake. That's—"

Bet patted Rose's thin hands, effectively cutting off the spate of nervous chatter. "Thank you for telling me, Rose. I..." She stood on rubbery legs. "I need to get Bonnie."

Tricia. Bet padded quietly through the grass, winding her way around the trunks of the pines. *Tricia*. She left the shade, and the sun struck hot on her face. Her eyelids narrowed against the glare, and she stumbled on while despair crept into her heart. The horror she had seen in Jake's eyes and the fury in his flushed face were all because of Tricia. Bet crossed her hands at her chest to rub the bruises on her upper arms. He had hurt her, because of... Tricia.

What had Tricia been like? What had she done to compel a love so strong that Jake could not bear to be reminded of her death even after so long a time?

Bet heaved a wistful sigh. She would never be able to compete with the ghost of his Tricia. She was a flesh-and-blood woman with faults and foibles. She would never be able to...

She lurched to a halt, blinking rapidly. Her hands pressed against her lips as though she had spoken those thoughts aloud and now must press them back again. What was she thinking? She didn't want to compete with his Tricia.

She took a step and stumbled. Looking down, she saw the rutted accordion-pleated tracks of tractor tires. A frown pinched at her brow, and her gaze rose with a lingering dread. Ahead was the hay barn, its rusty tin roof silhouetted against the fleecy sky. Why had she come here? Bonnie was waiting for her. She half turned, but her gaze strayed to the open loft door, and she vacillated between the potent pull of the calm reason her waiting daughter represented and the perplexing enigma of her desire to enter the barn, climb the ladder to the loft, and sit in that dark corner where she and Jake had found the scarifying heat of mindless passion.

No one was in sight. The tractor sat silently in the shade of the sweet gum trees' bright green, deep-toothed leaves. In the distance a horse whinnied. Nearer a flock of birds rose from the field as one, the rapid whooshing beat of their wings matching the rapid beat of her pulse.

She took one step, then another, moving toward the barn with the awkward gait of reluctance. The dim shadows bathed her in coolness. She breathed deep of the dusty smells of dirt and old cobwebs and dried hay. Her gaze glanced off the ladder even as her feet began to move toward it.

Climbing out onto the loft floor, she avoided the dark corner and trudged to a bale of hay. It made a prickly seat, but she was inured to any physical discomfort. Her hands lay slack atop her frosty yellow skirt. Her eyes stared blindly through the loft door toward the brick-red roof of Jake's house glinting through the pines in the distance.

Slowly the numb despair began to wear away. Her emotions came alive with the stinging pain of stabbing needles. Her fingers curled into her palms, and her lashes swept across her eyes like the fluttering wings of a butterfly. Breath swooped into her starved lungs, and her chest pumped rapidly while she fought an overwhelming, inexplicable urge to cry.

She had known all along that Jake still remembered his Tricia. Her framed portrait was tucked carefully into a lower drawer of his desk. Bet had seen him holding it once, his fingers caressing the cold glass surface. She had left him alone then. Alone with his thoughts and the sadness that hovered in his eyes.

She had her memories, too. Only . . . only John seemed so far away. His thin face was blurring like an old Polaroid improperly treated. The life they shared seemed so long ago. Almost . . . almost as if it had happened to someone else.

Hadn't it? Bet wondered distractedly. Weren't John's Elizabeth and Jake's Slugger two different people? The first a shy, unawakened girl, so easy and eager to please; the second a woman with a growing distaste for being satisfied with any crumbs of happiness life might offer. She knew from the beginning that this marriage was a substitute for what she and Jake had lost. His Tricia would always be first in his heart and thoughts, while she would be nothing more than a . . . a convenience. A means to a stable family. A . . . a baby factory!

Bet tried to swallow the taste of bitterness, but it met the upsurge of a soundless cry. Why was the idea so repugnant to her? Just weeks ago it was exactly what she wanted! Why did it hurt so much now? She dropped her face into her hands. The first trickle of tears was followed by a storm of sobbing.

Time slipped by on a stream of hot, salty tears. It was the creaking of a board that snapped her head up so rapidly her neck cracked. Jake stood beside the ladder, his dark face somber. She was instantly aware of a difference in him, some unfathomable change in the cloudy depths of his eyes.

The silence grew. The stillness deepened. The tears on her cheeks cooled and began to dry. One last tenacious crystalline drop trembled and fell, skimming down her flushed cheek. Jake looked away, and Bet's alert posture sank into a relieved slump.

"I heard you crying," he said, then stirred as though that was not what he meant to say.

"I'm sorry," Bet whispered hoarsely. His eyes returned to her, and she shivered slightly, twining her nervous fingers together. "Rose told me about—about the—the berries and your—your wife."

"You are my wife now."

The words were low and slow and measured, with an almost diffident quality that trod the fine line between question and statement. Yet Bet shrank from them. She felt the growing power of an amorphous, unknown threat, and her mouth went dry.

"Legally," she breathed, unable to find the strength to give the word any force. She heard the hissing intake of his breath and watched the ripple of his sun-browned skin over the tautening muscles along his jaw.

"Yes, legally," he bit out sarcastically. As though he could no longer bear to look at her, Jake threw his head back to stare up into the dusty, cobweb-coated rafters.

"It's—it's the way we wanted it," Bet said with a quaver of uncertainty.

His eyes rolled down, glittering at her across the tightening planes of his cheeks. He stared at her that way until she began to tremble; then his chin lowered and the hard glitter in his eyes softened. "It's what we wanted," he affirmed, but he sounded tired, almost defeated.

Bet felt the sting of fresh tears as he moved by her in an ambling walk. He stood in the loft door staring out. His booted feet were braced apart. His hands were thrust into the tight pockets of his faded jeans with his thumbs riding the waistband. The slanting sun carved him into two uneven halves like a crescent moon, one side bright, the other shadowed.

"I asked her to make me a cobbler that day."

It took a moment for that quietly emotionless statement to register with Bet. When it did, her stomach lurched sickeningly. "You blame yourself!"

"Yes."

"You shouldn't!" she cried out, aching for the guilt he must have flayed himself with through the years.

Silence. Thick, ominous silence.

Bet waited with every sense acutely, painfully alert. She pushed up from the cotton bale but was forced to wait until she could control her trembling legs. At his side she raised a slender hand to touch his upper arm. Through the cotton fabric she felt his slight quiver. "Tri—" The name, never before spoken aloud, stuck in her throat. "She—she wouldn't want you to do this to yourself."

He stared straight ahead. "The same thing could have happened to you today."

There was a strange, strangled quality in his voice, and Bet dropped her hand to her side. He didn't want her comfort. The thought was a painful one, and she felt a distance yawning between them. "I was careful," she murmured.

It was a whopping lie. She had clumped through the tall weeds with never a thought to what might be slithering underfoot and had plunged headlong into the briers in search of the fattest, juiciest berries, which always seemed to be in the tangled heart of the bushes.

Jake slanted a penetrating glance over his shoulder. "Why did you come to the loft, Bet?"

The unexpected question took her breath away. Her gaze dropped, and she nervously smoothed at her skirt with a suddenly sweating palm. "I don't know."

"Don't you?"

"No!" Her voice shrilled, and she swallowed hard. "No, I—I . . ." She edged away, succumbing to the impulse to look at the gloomy corner of the loft. Heat encompassed her wrist, and she looked down to find it trapped in Jake's hand.

"Why did you come to the loft?"

She tried to tug free, but he wouldn't let go. The formless threat rose about her again in a smothering fog of terror. She wrenched her wrist from his hand, stumbling back against a wall of bales. Her breath panted through her parted lips. "What difference does it make?" she cried.

"If you know the reason, then you know what difference it makes."

"But I don't! I don't! I don't..." *want to?* Bet bit her lip, her gaze straying to the corner with an expression of torment. Realization came like an agonizing blow and dragged a moan of denial from her. The formless threat took shape, and she knew, beyond any doubt, why she had come here. This was the only place she had felt Jake was completely her own! There had been no intrusions from the past. There had not been one crack in his singleminded concentration on her! He was hers, as he had never been before or since. For a few brief moments they had transcended past, present, and future. They were one, and the implication... Suddenly her sneakers were pumping across the rough loft floor, and she was scrambling down the ladder.

Jake made no effort to stop her. He turned back into the loft door to watch as she flew down the rutted tractor road, growing smaller and smaller, until she vanished in the dim shadows of the pines. His trapped breath sighed out unsteadily, and one shoulder sank toward the support of the door frame. Hopelessness wrinkled his brow into a frown.

Was he wrong? There were other reasons she could have come here. Privacy, for one. It didn't have to be a conscious or unconscious yearning for the one place they had shared an experience unique to them both.

He slid his fingers through his hair and kneaded the

back of his neck. God! He could still smell that cobbler. How could one simple, innocent dish change his life so drastically, not once, but twice? First, Tricia's death. Now . . .

When had it happened? Had it begun as early as that first kiss, when her lashes were clumped together in wet spikes and her eyes were luminous with tears? Was it the morning he leaned in through the bedroom doorway and watched her play This Little Piggy on Bonnie's toes? Or the first day she rode Rhapsody in a confident gallop, her face flushed with exhilaration?

Did it matter when it had happened? It had. He was in love with Elizabeth Valentine Calloway. His wife— legally!

8

THE MORNING WAS spiced with the aromas of baking apples, cinnamon, and toasted coconut. Bet stared into the grim gray twilight of the pre-dawn sky, watching the gay twinkling of a single star fade into the pewter-colored heavens. Was there such a thing as wishing on the last star of the night? If there was, what would she wish for? Her hand smoothed across her waist and down to her abdomen. A gently serene smile drifted across her mouth. A son, she thought. A healthy, happy son with his father's dark eyes and black hair. Should she tell Jake what she suspected or wait until it was confirmed?

The question shattered the tranquillity of her mood. It had been a week since she fled the hay barn and Jake. A week of wakeful nights and careful days. A week of waiting for the even rhythm of sleep to claim him while she stared dry-eyed into the darkness. A week of days with a minimum of conversation and a maximum of discomfort.

Her mind's eye filled with the image of Jake's face, dark and watchful as he slanted that penetrating look

107

over his shoulder and asked: "Why did you come to the loft, Bet?"

Did he know why? Did he understand the need that drove her? Did she?

The new glass pane caught the rays of the rising sun with a clean sparkle. Bet reached out, running a single finger across the lower edge of the frame, where a small dollop of putty had oozed up onto the glass. Jake had repaired it while she visited his mother one afternoon. What had he thought and felt while he worked on it? Had he remembered Tricia and the happiness they shared? Bet's hand dropped to her side. There were times when she hated this house. Tricia's house. Tricia's bed. Tricia's husband.

She sank into the chair at the table, resting her head in her hands. Jake would never be hers. Oh, there might be isolated moments snipped from the fabric of their lives. Moments when physical need scourged his mind of all else. Exhilarating, exciting moments when she would be allowed to give him what he needed, when she would be allowed to take from him all that he had to offer. Snippets of time—when she wanted it all.

Could she admit it now? She wanted what she had seen in the snapshot of Jake's parents. The one in which his father had his boot braced on the picnic bench, his elbow propped on his thigh. He and Mother Calloway were looking into each other's eyes with an expression of love and trust, their faces glowing with the contentment of a long and happy life. That was what she wanted: to grow old in grace and dignity and love. She wanted the youthful shine of inner contentment that contradicted the ravages of age on the outer shell. She wanted to love and be loved—and neither was possible.

She couldn't change the rules on Jake now. He had married her with certain expectations, and those had not changed. She couldn't allow herself to love him. It would embarrass him and humiliate her.

Bet looked down the long, lonely road her life would travel and knew that she had been wrong to deny the possibility of a new love. She would always treasure her memories of John, but he was gone and she was alive. It was an old cliché, but life did go on. She had been wrong to believe she could not survive the loss of another love. Love and loss were all part of life. It was time to crumble the barriers, to open her heart, to experience all that life had to offer.

"Bet?"

Jake stood at the opposite side of the table. A pair of hip-hugging jeans rode low on his bare torso. He was freshly scrubbed and combed, his hair still damp from the shower. He smiled, his lazy, sensual, early-morning smile that never failed to put spurs to her heartbeat.

"You didn't need to get up so early," she said, trying but failing to return his smile.

"That apple pie picked me up out of bed and floated me into the shower." One black eye vanished behind a slumberous wink. "Do you have to take it to the picnic today?"

Her laugh was genuine, a soft gurgle of amusement. "I made an extra one."

"With a tablespoon of vanilla, like you always do?" She nodded, and he sighed heavily. "I didn't know apple pies could be so good. Woman, you've found the way to my heart."

"Have I?" The question slipped from her before she thought, and once it was out she would have done anything to recall it. If it had been lightly teasing, she could have laughed it off. But it wasn't. It was deadly serious.

Jake stared at her, his smile fading. "Slugger..."

She popped from her chair, cutting him off. "I've always heard the way to a man's heart was through his stomach. Can I tempt you with fresh coffee?" She didn't wait or listen for an answer but hurried to the counter to begin pouring. Was it only a week ago she had tried to get to his thoughts through his stomach? And what a disaster that had been! She couldn't blame Jake. She had known from the beginning that there was a limit to what he was capable of giving. Steaming liquid sloshed over the side of the cup, and Jake was at her side, his hand covering hers to help her pour.

Together they set the coffee pot aside, and Jake's fingers curled into her hand. Her eyes lifted to meet his, and she saw the shadow of sadness that dulled the sheen of his black eyes. It hurt her to see it. It hurt worse to know that it had not been there before her surprise. She wished she had never heard of blackberries. She wished she had not reminded him of his Tricia and his grief.

Rationally she knew that the reminder could have come at any time and in any way: someone, something, some word that gave fresh life to the old grief. But there was little of rationality in her now. She was all raw nerves and chaotic confusion. Her eyes dropped to the hypnotic pulse in the hollow of his throat, and she felt the contraction of his hand around hers.

"Slugger, I . . ." he began and stopped. The pulse at his throat began to race. Her gaze was drawn up to meet his once more, and she discovered a confusion that matched her own. He swallowed hard, and his tongue slid nervously across his lips. "I . . ." The word died on a whisper of uncertainty.

She searched the liquid depths of his eyes but saw no answer to the puzzle of a Jake Calloway who was unsure of himself. Words swam to the surface of her memory. Words that were low and slow and measured. *You are my wife now.* Why did he say them? What did they mean?

Bet watched that curious inner struggle seesaw back and forth. She knew the moment impulse lost to reason, and the regret she saw in his face was mirrored in her own heart. What would he have said?

A frown tugged at his eyebrows, and he released her hand. He moved to the kitchen table, where he sank into the ladder-back chair and wrapped his hands around the cup. "We have to be up at the house at eight. Will you be ready?"

Bonnie bobbed along on Jake's shoulder, one tiny finger busy exploring his ear. He caught her hand between forefinger and thumb and grinned at her. "C'mon, Puddin'head, give Daddy a kiss." It was her latest trick. A wide, open-mouthed soggy buss on the lips or cheek. Jake puckered up, and Bonnie watched him with a round, blue-eyed stare while she mimicked the motion like a small bird.

Bet, following on the worn path that forked toward the farmhouse, smiled. Sometimes it was hard for her to remember that Bonnie was not Jake's daughter. The thought was not a new one, but the feeling that accompanied it was. The resentment was gone; in its place was a sense of peace. John would never be anything more to Bonnie than a picture in a dusty frame and a small fund of secondhand memories. It was right that Jake would be her reality of a loving father. He was the one who rocked her to sleep at night and rubbed her aching gums. He would be the one who kissed her skinned knees and terrorized her first beau. The image of Jake doing just that was so strong it made Bet laugh.

She looked ahead to the redbud tree with its heart-shaped leaves hanging limp in the searing heat. It seemed strange to her that Mother Calloway would want to begin the day with the added work of a family breakfast. The Fourth of July was not only a holiday; it was also the day for the yearly Calloway family reunion. Uncles, aunts, and cousins were coming from Arkansas, Texas, and South Louisiana, all bringing covered dishes to add to the cooking that had gone on for days in the Calloway Huddle.

Perhaps it wasn't so strange. The Calloways enjoyed working and playing together. As little experience as she had, Bet knew there was something special about them. A closeness and caring that few families achieved. And more—an acceptance and tolerance for both strengths and weaknesses in each other. She was fortunate to have met Aunt Hester and Jake and the Calloways, fortunate to have become a part of this family where love was more than a word. It was an active force in all of their lives.

She followed Jake up the back steps. He flung open the door and stepped aside for her to enter. A sea of expectant faces greeted her. Aunt Hester was there and, inexplicably, Carrie, with her brazen red hair and wide violet smile. Bet caught a glimpse of burning candles ringing the braided circle of a coffee cake.

"HAPPY BIRTHDAY!" The dull roar rolled over Bet, and she fell back a step, looking behind her to see if there was someone else.

Jake's hand rode her waist, his dark eyes somber as they gazed into hers. "Happy birthday, Slugger."

Bet swallowed a painful lump and blinked back tears. "I—I had forgotten," she said softly. "No one—no one has remembered since the—the Hunts." Her lip began to quiver, and she bit it, sucking in a deep breath. Jake held out his arm, and Bet threw herself against his chest, giving vent to the sob that welled up inside her. His lips grazed her forehead, and she felt a tugging on her white slacks. She looked down at Archie, her tears blurring his upturned face.

"Open my present first, Aunt Bet." He held up a small, soft package he had obviously wrapped himself.

"Archie, you shouldn't have."

"It's your birthday! Everybody got you something! C'mon, Aunt Bet, open it!"

She knelt down and began to tear the paper. Out fell a gaudy Archie handkerchief in garish shades of red and pink. She dared not glance up at Jake as she pulled Archie to her and gave him an enthusiastic hug. "It's beautiful."

He squirmed out of her arms and flung a look over his shoulder. "I told ya she'd like it! Mama wanted me to get you one with *flowers* on it," he said with disgust. "Hurry! You have to blow out your candles and open your presents!"

While everyone gathered around the table, Bet did as Archie ordered. The candles winked out, and the cake was taken away by Mother Calloway, who began slicing pieces and passing them around with coffee and juice. The hubbub of talk and laughter was accompanied by the crackling and tearing of wrapping paper and Archie's shrill suggestions about which present should be opened next. Jake leaned against the cabinet, a part of yet separate from the group. Bet's eyes met his with a happy glow when she unwrapped the western boots from him.

"Boots!" Aunt Hester snorted, her blue eyes frowning over her wire-rim glasses. "I hope you've done better by Bet than that, Jake Calloway!"

"But I love them, Aunt Hester," Bet protested, hugging them to her and lovingly tracing the intricate stitching. "They're beautiful! Thank you, Jake."

Unmollified, Aunt Hester snorted again. "Here." She dug through the pile of gifts. "Open this one from me. And Jake, you look at it! This is what a woman likes!"

Bet first set aside the lavender silk orchid buried in a royal purple bow and tore off the pink foil paper. Lifting the lid from the box, she folded back the tissue paper and gasped with pleasure. Flesh-colored lace with satin straps and bodice stared up at her. Expecting it to be a slip, she lifted it to a chorus of oohs and aahs from her sisters-in-law and Carrie. The soft folds tumbled out, and she found she was holding up—for *everyone's* inspection—a teddy cut high on the hips with bands of see-through lace.

Her wide gaze flew to Jake's face. His roguish grin and sparkling eyes brought the color flooding into her cheeks with burning warmth. Her hands snapped together, crushing the teddy, which she rolled up and stuffed into the box. "It's lovely, Aunt Hester," she said faintly, raising her cool hands to her hot cheeks.

"I'll thank you for that one, Aunt Hester," Jake called out.

In the burst of laughter that followed, Archie thrust another present into Bet's hands. "This one's from Uncle Jake, too."

She unwrapped a small book. It was old, the brown cloth binding was fraying on the corners, and the gilt lettering was wearing away on the spine. Opening it to the title page, she read aloud, "The Whip, Hoe, and

Sword; or, the Gulf Department in '63 by George H. Hepworth." Below the author's name was a quotation from Shakespeare: "This is all true as it is strange. Nay, it is ten times true; for truth is truth To the end of reckoning."

Truth is truth to the end of reckoning. And what was truth for her? Bet's unfocused gaze rose to Jake. *The truth.* She was in love with Jake Calloway. She loved the way his mouth promised a smile even in repose; she loved the way his thick mass of black hair sprang up away from his forehead. She loved the tenderness and thoughtfulness that was an innate part of him. She loved his strength and his laughter and his lovemaking. She loved him with a depth of emotion that had been lacking with John.

"Aunt Bet! This is an *old* book! Why would Uncle Jake give you an *old* book?"

It was so clear to her now. Why hadn't she realized it before? John hadn't wanted that from her. She had given him all he wanted: undemanding affection and companionship. Had there been a time when she wanted more from him? Had there been a moment of truth when she realized she must tailor her love to fit his needs? She couldn't remember, and it wasn't important anymore. All that was important was now and her and Jake and the love that suddenly swelled her heart within her breast.

"Aunt Bet, this book is *used!*"

Archie's outrage penetrated her thoughts, and Bet cupped his glossy black head with one hand, smiling gently at his indignant expression. "Can you read that, Archie? It was published in 1864. That makes it an antique."

"It's still *old!* Why didn't he get you a *new* book?"

"Because he knew that this one would make me much happier." There was a sweet caress in her voice as her eyes lifted to meet Jake's. She knew that her defenses were stripped bare, that her eyes glowed with the new-found knowledge of her love. She yielded to that impulse to open the floodgates of her heart until Jake jerked up, his eyes narrowing with an alert gleam. It was only then that she looked down and girded her thoughts.

"I will treasure it, Jake, always," she murmured, her glance sliding off him before she took the gift Archie pressed into her hands.

She laughed and traded quips with Pete. She unwrapped the last gift and gave a short speech thanking them all. She dabbed the perfume Carrie had given her behind her ears and those of her small, dark-haired niece. She ate coffee cake and drank coffee. And all the while her mind raced along a second level far away from the crowded, noisy kitchen.

Her eyes strayed to Jake again and again, as though he were a magnet she could not resist. She saw the puzzled expression in the dark eyes that followed her every move, and she knew he sensed a difference in her. That everyone else didn't seemed like a miracle. She felt different. She felt excited and elated and afraid. She wanted to laugh. She wanted to cry. She wanted to kick up her heels and shout for the pure joy of hearing her own voice. She felt young as she had never felt young before. She felt like a teenager in the throes of her first crush. Her skin prickled with suppressed excitement. Her heart raced. Her eyes glowed.

She wanted to be near Jake, to breathe in the manly scent of him, to touch the hard-corded thews of his forearms and marvel at the power concealed by his dark skin. But a strange sense of restraint kept her sandwiched between Aunt Hester and Carrie. She smiled. She laughed. She talked. Yet she was insensible to the conversation.

Bonnie slept on Jake's shoulder. Her thumb was tucked in her mouth, the fragile fan of her lashes resting on her cheeks. One dark hand encased her diapered bottom, the other moved in soothing circles over her back. Bet watched, her heart throbbing with a poignant thrill of happiness, as Jake rubbed his cheek gently over Bonnie's crown, disturbing the feathery topknot of strawberry curls caught up in a single tiny pink barrette. She had seen him do that many times, but never had it affected her so much. Her husband and her daughter—the two people she loved most in the world.

The party began to wind down. Pete and Burt left with their wives and children to begin preparations for the day. Father Calloway went to check on the beef revolving on the spit. Mother Calloway stirred the contents of the deep iron pots atop the stove, and Aunt Hester began chopping onions for the rice dressing. Bet sat at the table talking to Carrie, knowing that she should leave but paralyzed by the fear of being alone with Jake.

He crossed the kitchen, his every careless step bringing a corresponding leap of her pulse. "Bet, we need to get home."

"Of course." Bet flung him a nervous glance that failed to connect. "Carrie, you'll come with us?"

"Sure, honey. You gonna need somebody to help you carry all this stuff."

"I'll do that, if you'll take Bonnie," Jake offered.

"Oh, no!" Bet said a trifle sharply. If she took Bonnie, she would have to touch him. Somehow she couldn't bear to do that now. Not with people to watch them. "She might wake up. Why don't you go ahead. Carrie and I can bring everything."

For a moment she thought he would object, but he finally nodded an agreement and left.

After piling the gifts on Bet's bed, Carrie announced with her usual lack of delicacy that she needed to go to the john to freshen up. After all, she added, there might be some bachelors on the loose, and she'd taken a shine to the Calloway men.

Alone, Bet lifted her book from Jake, absently rubbing the nubby texture of the cover. A dreamy smile tipped the corners of her mouth up.

"You look happy." Jake stood in the doorway, one hand braced high on the sill, the other tucked into the pocket of his jeans.

The dreamy smile blossomed to radiance. "I am," she

said simply. "Thanks. No one has ever remembered except the Hunts and you."

"Not even...John?"

She turned away, her fingers squeezing tightly around the edges of the book. "Oh, John thought birthdays were for children."

"There's some child in all of us."

"I suppose there is. Do you think we ever really grow up?"

"I hope not."

Bet looked at him and smiled. "It would be a shame, wouldn't it?"

"Yes," he said, his eyes riveted to her face. "Look at Archie. He doesn't know the meaning of the word *fear*. He expects everyone to be good to him. He expects everyone to love him. He hasn't learned yet that love can be offered and rejected, wanted and withheld."

Offered and rejected. The cold light of reason froze the happy mists of Bet's dream. "There is that," she said tightly, her eyelids dropping to shield her stricken expression. She moved to the dresser with jerky movements and laid the book down, one shaking hand caressing it. She'd been so caught up in her own feelings that she'd forgotten Jake wouldn't return them. He had given her so much, but there was a limit. She would have everything she had with John. Affection, companionship. But it wasn't enough. With Jake it wasn't enough.

"Slugger"—Jake's hand touched her shoulder—"look at me."

She averted her face, stubbornly refusing. Her happiness had been shattered too quickly. She couldn't control the trembling of her lips, and she knew her eyes would betray the utter desolation she felt.

But Jake was not to be thwarted. He turned her to him and hooked one forefinger beneath her chin, raising her face. "Slugger, there was a minute this morning when you looked at me and I thought...I thought I saw..."

The unsteady tremor of his voice trailed off, and Bet

lifted her lashes slowly. She saw his square chin and the uneven, grimacing line of his mouth and his nose with white flaring nostrils and his frowning eyes. What a fool she had been to give herself away like that! It wasn't only embarrassment Jake felt; it was anger. She had been right. The rules were made; they couldn't be changed. She swallowed hard and stared at the erratic pulse in his throat.

"I . . . I don't know what you mean." Was that her voice? So calm, so light and unaffected by the pain that was ripping at her?

His hand dropped. He swiveled to the wall behind him, raising his forearm and leaning his brow against it. The pose astonished Bet, holding as it did an air of dejection. Surely she was wrong. It was the anger that bowed his shoulders and drew his hands into fists. Still, she couldn't leave him like that.

"Jake?"

He straightened abruptly, a dull flush climbing his neck and stealing across his face. "I, uh, I have to go help Dad mop the beef."

Bet was at a loss. "Mop the beef?"

"Yeah. We have a huge tub of barbecue sauce and a real honest-to-God mop to baste the meat." The ghost of his old smile glimmered. "And I don't want you anywhere near that mop. I haven't forgotten how handy you are with one."

It was his stupid pride, Jake thought with a scowl. Lord, when she looked at him that morning he would have sworn what he saw was love. It was all he could do to keep himself from going to her there in the midst of everyone and demand that she tell him. Did he want it so badly he was imagining it? Why didn't he just ask? All she could say was no. And no was what he couldn't stand to hear. Jake Calloway had his useless, stupid pride!

The family reunion was in full sway. A mess of half-eaten meals covered the long row of picnic tables beneath a cloud of buzzing flies lighting atop covers and napkins thrown over bowls and pots and pans. The sun glared from the colorless sky, burning all moisture from the dusty air, and the chattering groups that melted and reformed in a constant pattern were filled with men and women fanning themselves with paper plates, napkins, and hats—anything that was handy and would stir a cooling breeze. A desultory softball game with players from six to sixty was in progress, and horseshoes rang against iron rods in the shade of the chinaberry tree.

Jake stood apart in the same posture he had assumed just months before. One scuffed cowboy boot was propped on the low-cut stump, his forearm resting on his thigh. It had been comfortably warm that day, but now the hot sun beat through the blue plaid of his western shirt and sweat rolled down the identation of his spine. Other than a slight twitching of his shoulders when the beading sweat tickled, he paid no attention to the broiling heat.

His thoughts were on that other day when he had stood in the same spot in the same way. Then loneliness had eaten at him, making him feel set apart from the couples he matched. Then he had thought himself incapable of loving again. But then he hadn't known Bet.

He searched the yard and found the impossibly glaring red of Carrie's hair. Peeping beyond her shoulder he saw Bet's cap of bronze hair glinting with red and gold lights. She moved, and he saw her laugh, and he knew that her small tilted nose would be wrinkled with amusement, her eyes sparkling with gentle humor. She adjusted the sleeping Bonnie in her arms, and Jake moved, stepping away from the stump.

A minute later he was at her side, one of a group of women clustered around ninety-year-old Great-grandma Calloway, who sat in a rocker with a shawl around her shoulders and a throw across her knees, querulously complaining it was too cool to be outside.

"Here, Bet," he murmured beneath the chatter. "Bonnie's too heavy for you to hold this long."

"She *is* beginning to feel like a ton of bricks."

Her smile was strained, and her light voice had a

weary drag to it. Jake frowned down at her while the transfer was made. For a moment his attention was on Bonnie, who fretted irritably and rubbed her fist across her snub nose before squirming around to find her comfortable spot. Her thumb dug into the side of her lip before slipping into her mouth. She sucked once, twice, and sighed heavily before falling back to sleep.

With Bonnie settled, he turned his attention to Bet. She was pale, the sprinkling of freckles dusting her cheeks standing out in stark relief. She looked exhausted. Her eyelashes drooped as though they were too heavy for her. Her attempt to concentrate on the conversation flowing back and forth was an obvious effort.

Jake put his arm around her waist and pulled her to him, ducking his head close to her ear. "Slugger, are you all right?"

"Sleepy," she murmured, stifling a yawn and nuzzling her cheek against his chest. "Ate too much. Heat. Sleepy."

Jake grinned and kissed the top of her head. "Ladies, if you'll excuse us? I've got to put my two girls down for a nap."

"No," Bet murmured, struggling to lift her head. "Carrie . . ."

"Honey, you don't worry about me. You see that poor, unsuspecting soul over yonder?" She paused while Jake and Bet followed the line of her pointing finger. Jake's cousin, Richard, sat in solitude on a lawn chair beneath the pines, puffing contentedly on a pipe. "Well, I've learned he's a footloose and fancy-free Calloway. Looks kinda lonesome, don't he? Think I'll mosey over and keep him company." Carrie's wide mouth inched into a cheerful smile, and the long sweep of her false lashes dipped in a wink.

As she sauntered off with a languorous swing of her hips, Jake chuckled. "Richard won't know what hit him."

Bet stifled another yawn and leaned her cheek against his chest. "Carrie might be good for him. The few times I've tried to talk to him, he just puffed on his pipe and nodded his head."

"That's Richard." Jake laughed. As he led Bet away, Jake saw Aunt Hester following them with an expression that combined satisfaction and anticipation. The satisfaction he understood. But what was the anticipation?

He was still wondering when he laid Bonnie atop the crib mattress. She opened one blue eye. A smile veed away from the hip of her thumb, the feathery furl of her lashes settled back to her cheek, and she was asleep again without fuss or bother.

Jake hung over the crib, one knuckle tracing the downy curve of her cheek. "I love you, Puddin'head," he whispered, and her tiny smile came and went as though she had heard and understood his words. He thought of the comment his mother always made when a baby smiled in its sleep. Talking to the angels. That was his Bonnie, an angel. He couldn't imagine his life without her or that other angel across the hall. He leaned down to kiss the pink shell of Bonnie's ear before leaving.

Bet was just slipping beneath the covers. Jake noted the haphazard pile of clothes dropped to the floor and realized she must really be tired. His neat Bet never scattered her clothes.

"I'm so sorry to do this in the middle of the reunion, Jake," she murmured. "But I can't seem to keep my eyes open."

He sat on the edge of the bed, bracing one arm across her. "Sleep. Don't worry about it."

Her eyes were closed, her breathing even. "Shouldn't leave guests," she sighed, curling away from him with her hands tucked beneath her cheek.

The minutes ticked away while Jake sat and watched her sleep. At length he leaned down to kiss her bare shoulder. He opened his mouth and closed it. A muscle began jumping in his jaw. Even when she was asleep and couldn't hear him, he could not say the words aloud. He couldn't tell her he loved her. He couldn't ask if she loved him. He couldn't assure her that her grief for John would end one day, and she would then be ready to reach out and grab hold of life. He couldn't promise that he would be waiting and hoping she would yield to him the heart she so zealously guarded.

He stood and stared down at her, his black eyes soft with yearning. He had a lifetime to win her. If he didn't, he would have a lifetime of regret. He left her with a last lingering look that mingled hope and despair.

Jake slitted his eyes against the brilliance of the sunlight as he strolled across the yard. Aunt Hester detached herself from the fringe of the crowd and hurried toward him. Her broad smile crinkled the soft crepey skin of her cheeks, and her blue eyes twinkled mischievously over the gold rims of her glasses, perched as always on the button of her nose.

"Jake Calloway, I'm furious with you!" But she didn't look furious. The white bun atop her crown bobbed up and down, and the bright sparkle of her eyes seemed to come from deep within her. "Why didn't you tell me?"

"Tell you what?" he asked curiously.

"That Bet's pregnant!"

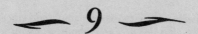

9

THE ROOSTER CROWED, and Jake's eyes popped open. A moment later the corners of his mouth climbed in a rueful smile. Anyone watching would have thought he had wakened suddenly—a far cry from the truth. He had spent a miserable night, neither asleep nor awake, while his thoughts twirled on a merry-go-round that refused to submit to the deadening effects of sleep.

Bet was nestled against him. Her updrawn knees and shins were molded to his thigh, her toes tucked beneath his knee. Her forehead pressed against his shoulder, and her hand lay lax across the crook of his elbow. She had slept through afternoon, evening, and night, not stirring when he crawled into bed, undisturbed by his restless tossing.

A fragile blue vein beat sluggishly in her temple. Jake studied it, aching to reach out and brush his finger across it. But he was afraid he would wake her. If he did, he would have to look deep into the tawny splendor of her eyes. He would begin to search for some sign, however

123

small and insignificant, of the love he thought he had seen.

He raised his free arm, pillowing his head in his hand. Staring sightlessly at the ceiling, he remembered how Aunt Hester had laughed at his slack-jawed amazement, saying: *"Don't tell me she hasn't told you!"*

"No, she hasn't, and I don't understand how you could be so sure."

"Because she's so sleepy!"

He pressed his fingers to the ache that began drawing between his brows. "What does that have to do with it?"

"She did the same thing when she was carrying Bonnie."

The feeling of helplessness and ignorance irritated him. Hell, what did he know about pregnant women! "I thought she would get sick and throw up all the time."

"Some women do, not all. Bet never got sick. She just needed an inordinate amount of sleep. Of course, I could be wrong, Is this the first time she's napped in the afternoon?"

"I . . . uh . . . actually, no." He had found her napping three times in the last week or so. Did that really mean . . .

"Congratulations!" Aunt Hester beamed. "I've never known Bet to take a nap when she wasn't pregnant."

Jake dragged his hand from beneath his head and rested his coiled fist atop his brow. Pregnant. Was Bet really expecting his child? If she was, where was the elation and excitement he expected to feel?

Though he tried to dredge it up, all he felt was a faint tingling of regret. He wanted children. That was why they had married in the first place. But not yet. It was too soon. There was too much unresolved. He needed more time.

Legally. The word whispered with a malevolent hiss. They were bound by religious and temporal vows, not by ties of the heart. Bet had made it very clear what she wanted of their marriage: home, children, safety, security. She affirmed that her feelings had not changed with that single word—*legally.*

In the beginning he, too, thought he knew what he wanted. He thought then that he would not change, would not forget, would not grow. But he had. It was sheer stupidity to think that he and Bet could stand still. His feelings had changed. His needs had changed. And Bet's? What of hers? Had she stood still? Did she see him as nothing more than the means to an end?

God, why had she looked at him like that? Her image was so vivid, as if it had been seared into his memory with a branding iron. Her lips slightly parted. Her cheeks flushed. Her eyes wide and wondering and flooded with . . . what?

If only he could know for sure. Time. He needed time. He couldn't risk destroying the delicate balance of affection that had been forged in their brief marriage. He couldn't rush Bet before she was ready. He couldn't tell her that he loved her, but he could show her. With patience and perseverance, he could build the shelter of his love brick by brick. Then he would invite her in.

Beside Jake, Bet woke slowly, swimming lethargically through progressively lighter layers of sleep. For a time she sensed more than felt his presence. Warmth and contentment and a strange kind of happiness oozed through her veins with the sweetness of warm clover honey. Her eyelids fluttered open. The delineated muscles of Jake's upper arm were at the end of her nose. She resisted the impulse to nip it, just to see if it tasted as good as it looked. Smiling to herself, she moved her head back onto the pillow to study his profile.

"Morning," she said softly, her voice gentle and loving.

Jake rolled his head toward her, peering from the shadow of his fist. "Morning. How are you feeling?"

His deep, textured voice caressed her, and Bet's happiness surged with the giddy potency of a strong wine. "Wonderful!" she exclaimed, her nose wrinkling between a sunny smile and sparkling eyes. She stretched and yawned and wriggled into the pillow like a playful kitten, then climbed onto an elbow and smiled down at him.

His lazy smile was at odds with his dark, guarded expression. It puzzled her for a moment, until the events of the previous day came echoing back. She loved him. That was the source of the happiness that throbbed with a sensation akin to pain. Love. A beautiful, precious gift not to be squandered or cast aside. She could elect to hoard it like a miser, waiting for the assurance of some return, or she could share it. She could give Jake the gift of her heart without the words he didn't want to hear.

Her smile assumed a sprightly air. "Have I ever told you how handsome you are?"

"No," he said seriously, "I don't think you have."

"Should I?"

"I won't object."

Her hand rested on the shallow valley centering his chest, and she felt the warmth of his skin and the slow, methodic thud of his heart. "I wouldn't want to swell your head."

He uncoiled his fist and slipped his hand beneath his head, his elbow winging out along the pillow. "Swell it, woman, swell it," he chuckled through the widening smile that creased the bronze planes of his cheeks.

Bet arched over the arm lying along his side, tucking it behind her, and tried to concentrate as his wayward hand began roaming across her back and down her hip.

Jake arched a brow. "I'm waiting."

"You're distracting me," she complained, wishing she hadn't when his roving hand ceased its exploration. Pursing her lips in a pout, she veiled her eyes with her lashes. "You listen too well."

"Your wish is my command." He once again dragged his nails gently over the slithery fabric of her apricot gown, the combined slide and scrape sending chills radiating from her hip.

Bet shivered. "Is it?"

"Is it what?"

"Your command."

"Always," he answered, his eyes bright with laughter.

"Then," she drawled, unable to look into his eyes as she traced the curvature of his lower lip with the tapered tip of one finger, "prepare to be seduced."

"Seduced?" he asked with a surprised, husky growl.

"Um-hmm." She nodded, trailing her finger down his chin and across the column of his neck to the pulsing vein that leaped into high gear at her touch. She chanced a glance and found a smile frolicking at the corners of Jake's mouth even while he swallowed hard.

"I think I'm going to like this," he said, the merest tremor in his voice betraying the lightness of his tone, and then he settled his head into the pillow and closed his eyes.

Bet stared at him for a moment, perplexed by this reaction. "What are you doing?"

The lush fan of lashes climbed over one eye. "I'm preparing myself. After all, I've never been seduced before."

"You haven't?" A thread of excitement fluttered in her voice.

"Never." It was a solemn pronouncement, but the pulsing vein leaped against the light weight of her finger, and his black eyes burned into hers with an intensity that forced her gaze down.

She watched, seemingly absorbed by the movement of her hand across his flesh. Her palm skimmed up the length of his collarbone to the cap of his shoulder and out along the rigid muscles of his upper arm. A darting glance slanted through the screen of her lashes, and she sighed softly. "We have a problem."

"Do we?" The question floated on a shuddering breath.

She retraced her path to the center of his chest and began to make leisurely circles in the wiry matting of black hair. "Yes." Bet stopped to clear the quiver of rising passion from her voice. There was something incredibly erotic about having him lie so still. His every muscle was rigid, his breathing erratic. Each time she lifted her hand she could sense him waiting, suspended on the aching moments until she touched him once more.

She laid her hand flat on his chest, pressing gently, and heard the sigh of expelled air. She tried to smile, but her stiff lips would not move. Her eyes climbed slowly to meet his. "You see," she whispered, "I've never seduced a man before."

"I . . ." Jake choked off on a gasp when she curled her fingers and began to drag her nails down his chest, leaving a spreading wake of clamoring goosebumps. "I, ah, can see where that might be a problem."

Tempting, teasing fingers danced around his navel, and Jake's breath left him on a small huff of sound. Bet licked her lips at his tight, pained expression and tried, unsuccessfully, to dampen the excitement that was raging through her. Her hand dropped lower, her nails tracing the band of his shorts, and his chest swelled on an indrawn breath that slowly dribbled out between his clenched teeth. Bet met his hot eyes with a wide gaze of assumed innocence. "How will I know if I'm doing it right?"

He tried to smile and failed. He tried to speak and couldn't. At last his lips moved. "So far, so good."

"Think so?" she asked breathlessly, her heart pounding in her throat. She could feel the soft cotton of his shorts against the heel of her hand and the heat of his skin burning her fingertips. And she knew she had started something she couldn't finish. She wanted him desperately. Her body was alive with sensations, her every cell quivering, a separate and distinct entity yearning for him.

A wash of shame and dismay brought stinging heat to her cheeks. She had gone this far; she couldn't back down now. She was a woman, not a child. And Jake wasn't John. This was a different man, a different relationship, a different attitude. She couldn't fail him or herself. She loved him. She wanted to share that love in all of its meanings.

She steeled herself, squeezing her eyes shut. One finger gingerly dipped beneath his waistband.

Her world reeled. Before she knew what was happening, she was flat on her back. Her eyes flew open. Jake leaned over her. His eyes were glazed with passion, but laughter rumbled from deep in his chest.

"I should have just lain there to see what you would do."

"You knew that I—I . . ."

"Had gone as far as you could? Yes, I knew." His lips moved on hers with the softness of velvet. "Slugger, what am I going to do with you?"

Tears pooled in her eyes and slipped across her temples. "I want to . . . to make you happy."

"Bet, you don't have to do anything to make me happy. Being who and what you are does that. I like you just the way you are. Sweet and innocent and seductive."

"But, Jake—"

"Ssh." His thumb scrubbed gently at her frown. "Don't worry about it, Bet. We have a lifetime to get you used to me. It doesn't have to all happen now. It can be like reading a book. Every day is a new page, a new discovery."

Bet twined her arms around his neck and pulled his head down. The kiss was endless. His firm, hungry lips devoured hers. His tongue dipped into the moist recesses of her mouth, searching and tasting until she trembled beneath him.

He drew back with a fierce light in his eyes, and his hand left the curve of her cheek to steal down to her breast, where he teased the taut peak with his thumb. "Now," he said raggedly, "I'd like to finish what you started."

And he did, with a thoroughness that left Bet breathless and shaken. Through the mindless haze of soaring passion seeped a dim awareness of a difference in his lovemaking. It was in his hands—the wonderful, sensitive hands that tortured her with pleasure. It was in his eyes—the liquid black eyes that blazed with some inner flame that defied comprehension. It was in his lips—the lips that touched and tasted and thrilled her until she moaned aloud. It was in his face—his beautiful face with dark, sunburned skin drawn tight over the bold, strong bone structure. It shimmered like a gossamer web—

a subtle, elusive, tantalizing nuance on an old theme.

He had always been relentlessly absorbed in the physical act that hovered so perilously near love, but never had she felt like a pagan goddess tenderly arrayed upon an altar for the solitary worship of one man.

She didn't know when she began to cry the silent tears that skimmed across her temples and dampened her hair. It was only afterward that she learned. Jake lay atop her, his weight braced on his forearms. His chest heaved with the effort to drag air into his lungs, and his mellow, smiling gaze caressed her. She saw the shade of a frown and felt his finger touch her temple and saw him stare at it before his eyes plumbed hers with a question rimmed with hurt. She tried to smile, but there were no reassuring smiles in her. There was only a vast, vibrating well of love that grew by the minute.

"Because it was . . . beautiful," she whispered, and she saw the hurt wither and wondered at the dazzling light that took its place.

"Slugger," he rasped before claiming her mouth. His lips were soft, gently moving upon hers as though he would memorize every contour and curve. She sensed the clinging reluctance as their lips parted and he raised his head. "There's something I need to tell you."

He didn't finish. Bet waited. His curious tension communicated itself to her, and her hands tightened on his sweat-slicked ribs. "Yes?"

The dazzling light died down to a dim flame and winked out. A frown creased his brow and tugged at the corners of his mouth, and his eyes turned an impenetrable obsidian black.

The silence was thick with unspoken questions until it was shattered abruptly by Bonnie's rising wail. Jake's head jerked up as he cocked an ear to listen. The wail became a full-throated scream, and his eyes met Bet's and danced away. She felt the release of his tension in the slackening muscles beneath her hands.

"Polite little thing, isn't she?" Jake said lightly. "She waited till we were finished."

"Were we?" Bet asked, trying to capture his shifting gaze.

He moved from her, sliding off of the bed and reaching for his jeans. "Don't get up; I'll get her."

Bet's eyes followed him. The deep valley of his spine ended with a feathering V of downy black hair. She knew it was softer to the touch than the crisp hairs on his chest that clutched at her fingers and wrapped around them as though they didn't want to let her go. He disappeared through the doorway, and she sighed. Someday she would be able to trail butterfly kisses down the length of his spine and bury her lips in the deep hollow at his waist and dance her curious fingers aross the firm, flat buttocks that taunted her from the shelter of his jeans. Someday she would be the tigress, and he would be her prey.

Bonnie's crying stopped, and Bet heard her daughter's gurgling laughter and the soft murmur of Jake's voice. Someday, she thought with a reflective smile, she would shed her old inhibitions, and then she would make Jake Calloway quiver right to his marrow.

"Pee-yuu! Stinky diaper!"

Jake's exclamation shot across the hall, and Bet clapped a hand over her mouth to stifle a giggle. Eyes shining with merriment, she sat up to plump the pillows. Relaxing against them, she listened to the low murmur of his voice.

He was everything and so much more than she had imagined a man could be. Jake, with his wholesome acceptance of his body and hers, had given her the freedom to explore the intricacies of her femininity and his masculinity. But something held her back. What?

"Bet?"

Jake stood at the side of the bed with Bonnie in his arms. She saw the concern on his face and knew, suddenly, that a deep and lightless chasm yawned between the act of love and the act of sex. Sex, no matter how physically satisfying, could never substitute for a multifaceted love involving heart and mind, soul and body. She would never be truly free with Jake, not while he rejected her heart and kept his own closed against her.

She smiled, a frail smile tinged with sadness, and raised her arms for Bonnie, who kicked her sturdy legs and tried to jump out of Jake's arms. Bet folded her wriggling daughter to her and breathed deeply of baby powder and that fresh, clean smell that belonged so uniquely to a baby.

"I'll put the coffee on and come back."

Jake's last word hovered on the hesitant lip of a question, almost as though he thought she wouldn't want him to return. Bet settled Bonnie against the support of her updrawn thighs and caught his hand, drawing its darkly furred back to her cheek. "Do," she said softly, holding his brooding gaze. "We'll have a lazy morning."

"Sounds good." He turned his hand and caressed her cheek, then hurried out.

Bonnie watched him go, feathery tufts of pale strawberry curls floating as she swiveled her head. Her small face puckered in a frown, and her lower lip began to tremble. "Uh, uh, uh," she grunted, her dimpled arm stretching out with flexing fingers. Fat tears welled in her deep blue eyes and plunged down her cheeks. Her small mouth yawned wide, revealing the sharp edges of two tiny teeth. Before she could let go with an all-out squall, Bet snapped her fingers at the tip of Bonnie's snub nose.

Her expression of blinking astonishment was so comical Bet had to laugh, even though she would have preferred to squall along with her. Another sign of her likely pregnancy. Tears never seemed far from the surface. She'd have to tell Jake soon, but first she wanted to know for sure.

Bonnie was not to be thwarted. She might be tiny and rosy and cuddly, but she had a mind of her own. Once the initial surprise passed, she screwed her small round face into a close approximation of a gargoyle and let go with an ear-splitting scream. Bet sighed and pulled her across her chest, where Bonnie rooted around, ignoring her soothing murmurings. Crying as if her heart were broken, she turned her small face to the door and stretched out her hand.

"He'll be back soon, sweetie," Bet promised.

And he was. Jake came barreling through the door. "Is she hurt?"

"No, she wanted you to come back."

"Did she?" He grinned, clearly delighted, and crawled onto the bed. Sinking one elbow into the pillow, he propped his head on his hand. "Are you giving your mama a hard time, Puddin'head?"

Bonnie's crying stopped with the rapidity of a faucet being turned off. One glistening tear dripped from her cheek as she chortled gleefully and caught his proffered finger. Holding it in a death grip, she squirmed around on Bet's chest until she was comfortable, tucked her thumb into her mouth, and began drifting off to sleep. Every few seconds one blue eye would spring open and she would give Jake an angelic smile around the impediment of her thumb before the fragile furl of her lashes floated back to her damp cheeks.

"She loves you," Bet whispered.

Jake's eyes met hers. "I love her. God, there's nothing like it, is there? I always thought I knew how I'd feel, but I didn't know the half of it. On top of the world and scared to death at the same time."

"I can't imagine you being scared of anything."

"Can't you?"

Bet didn't know whether it was the gritty sound of his voice or the leaping flame in his eyes that made her so intensely aware of his hand lying along the outer curve of her breast with Bonnie's trusting grip on one extended finger.

"Take Bonnie," he continued. "Just looking at her can terrify me. There are so many things a parent can do wrong."

"You'll be gray before she blows out her first candle if you keep thinking like that. Just love her, Jake; that's all she needs." Stricken by a sudden niggling doubt, Bet looked away. Her hold upon Bonnie firmed with a fierce protectiveness. "Do you . . . do you think you'll feel different about your own child?"

A taut quality sharpened the air like the tangy acrid taste of ozone heralding the approach of a summer storm. Slowly her head turned, and her gaze plunged into the black moonless night of his eyes.

"In my heart, Bonnie is my own. There will be no difference."

"I'm glad," she whispered. "I'm—I'm glad."

He continued to watch her with his darkling eyes as though he expected her to say more. There was an element of vigilance in his alert posture that sent a current of unease rippling across the surface of Bet's peace. She felt she should say something more but didn't know what. Soon Jake's finger twitched against her breast, and his bated breath flowed on a deep, almost distressed sigh.

"Bet, is there something you wanted to tell me?"

She heard the strain in his voice and searched his face for some clue to its origin. "No, there . . ." She paused. "There is something, Jake. I . . . I'd like to go away for a few days."

Blank surprise was followed by a volatile array of emotions before the last restless frown smoothed away. Jake gave her a hollow smile. "We can take our honeymoon. Anywhere you want to go. New Orleans? You'd love going through the Confederate Museum. Or—"

"No," Bet interrupted. "I meant . . . alone. Well, not exactly alone. I thought I'd drive Aunt Hester back to Shreveport and spend a week or so with her. I really didn't get to visit with Carrie yesterday. And I do need to take Bonnie to visit her grandparents. It wouldn't be fair for her or them if I allow them to grow apart." But the most important reason she kept to herself: a visit to her doctor and a test.

His thumb grazed Bonnie's tiny pink fingers. "No, of course it wouldn't."

"Jake?" She touched his cheek. "It's only a week. I'll be back." She didn't know what impelled her to say it, but she was glad she had.

He gave her his old teasing smile. "If you don't, I'll be coming after you."

The following morning Jake stood in the drive watching the powder-blue Sentra vanish down the gravel road in a cloud of dust. His only consolation for the loneliness that settled around him like a shroud was Bet's last clinging kiss and the soft words she whispered against his cheek: "I'll miss you, Jake."

He hugged them to him like a talisman through the long hot day he spent cutting hay with his father and brothers. It was dark when he came home to his empty house. There was no Bonnie to come scooting across the floor with her peculiar swimming crawl, her head raised, and her round eyes shining. There was no Bet to come rushing out of the kitchen with a wooden spoon in her hand and a welcoming smile brightening her every delicate feature.

He flicked on the light and looked around the room and listened to the silence. A bead of sweat trickled across his forehead. He swiped at it and cursed, a low, hard sound that was swallowed by the silence and lost as though it had never been.

The hushed thump of his boots on the floor was an alien sound that intruded on the stillness. He stripped and showered, scrubbing away the sweat and dust of his labor. Dried and dressed in fresh jeans and T-shirt, he wandered into the bedroom, at a loss as to what to do with himself. If Bet and Bonnie were there...

They weren't, he reminded himself as he lifted Bet's perfume and sniffed the flowery fragrance. Strolling to the nightstand, he found the book he had given her for her birthday. Just seeing it there gave him an odd measure of comfort. It waited for her as he did, and she would return to them both.

In Bonnie's room he fingered the jar of petroleum jelly and the tube of Desitin ointment, then went to the crib and wrapped his hands around the rail. A soft percale sheet covered the mattress with a neatly folded blanket at one end. Jake rubbed his hand across it and found it cool to the touch, without the warmth that lingered from Bonnie's small, cuddly body.

He made a sandwich he couldn't eat and went to his study to work. Sinking down into the chair at his desk, he stared at the neatly typed pages of his manuscript and listened, once more, to the ominous silence that brooded in the empty rooms. Stirring himself from those fanciful thoughts, Jake flipped through the stack of books and found pages marked with strips of paper covered with notes jotted in Bet's small firm hand. He pulled his note-pad toward him and reached for a pencil, but a memory caught him with a sudden piercing sweetness, and his hand hovered in midair.

Bright sunlight slanted off the beating wings of memory to pour across the desk. He could see the lacy pink briefs draped across the pencil jar like a weary umbrella. He could see Bet's bronze hair turned to glowing red embers, and he remembered the erotic dance of love performed on couch and rug.

He knew he would never be able to work. He couldn't stay in that cold, lonely, empty house. It shocked him, that driving need to escape. He had suffered through loneliness and emptiness after Tricia's death. He had survived elastic hours that stretched in eternal solitude. He had known, then, that Tricia would never return to him, and he had stayed in that house, alone, for the days that turned to weeks and years. He knew now that Bet would be back in the short space of a week, yet he couldn't bear the glaring sound of forsaken silence. He rose slowly and forced himself not to run.

A frail sickle moon rose behind Jake as he followed the trail to his parents' back door. He found his mother washing dishes and his father sitting at the table reading the newspaper with a tall glass of iced tea nearby.

"Jake!" His mother's eyes dropped to the canvas over-night bag dangling from the end of his hand. "We didn't expect to see you."

"I, uh..." He studied the toes of his boots, feeling more than a little ridiculous. Here he was, thirty-four years old, a husband and father in every way that counted, running home like a scared kid. "I wondered if I could ...could stay with ya'll while Bet's gone."

The newspaper rattled and fluttered as it was folded. "Son, you know you're welcome here any time."

"It'll be nice having you," his mother added as she briskly dried her hands. "This big old house can get mighty lonesome for Dad and me since you boys got your own places."

Jake gave her a slow, grateful smile. "I would have thought it stayed a little too lively with all of us here in your hip pocket."

She laughed and nodded toward a chair. "I'll get you a glass of tea."

He set his bag by the door and settled into a chair. The radio hummed in the background with oldies but goodies, and cubes of ice plinked and crackled in the glass. There was comfort here, but more important, there was life.

"Nice night," he said to his father. "It's cooled off some."

"Yep, but we can expect another scorcher. We ought to finish cutting the hay tomorrow, then we can start bailing along about—"

"Here's your tea," his mother interrupted. She rested her hand on the swell of his shoulder. "Want to talk about it?"

"Now, Esther, he'll talk when he's ready. No sense in rushing a man's fences."

"Shoo! Listen to him!" she chided with fond disdain. "He chews a problem like a cow with a cud! As many ways as I want you to be like your father, *that* isn't one of them! So spit it out. You'll feel better."

Jake trailed a finger across the sweat beading the side of his glass. "Aunt Hester thinks Bet's pregnant."

"Hester thinks?"

"Because she's been so sleepy. I guess she was like

that with Bonnie. I don't know, though. Bet hasn't told me."

His mother sank into the chair at his side. "She could be waiting till she's sure. Bet knows how much you want a baby. She might not want to get your hopes up for a false alarm."

Jake continued to toy with his glass. "I guess so."

"That isn't the problem, is it?"

He gave her a lopsided grin. "No, it isn't."

"Well?"

He sucked in a deep breath and expelled it slowly. "I love her."

"We've been wondering when you were going to realize that," Esther Calloway chuckled. "Don't look so surprised! We'd have to be blind not to see it!"

Jake looked to his father, who laughed aloud. "Son, for such a smart man, you've really been lag-footed on this one."

"I can't argue with that." Jake's slow smile turned to laughter. A sudden rush of happiness warmed him. He'd said the words. Maybe not to Bet, but he'd said them—and it hadn't hurt a bit! "You know, I keep trying to figure out when it happened, but I can't."

"That's because it grew slowly," his mother said as she patted his hand. "Somewhere along the way liking turned into love, and that's the best kind."

"Yes, I think it must be," he said softly.

"And you!" His mother had a touch of asperity that reminded him of his Aunt Hester. "You're more like your father than I thought! We could be all night dragging this out of you. So far you haven't told us a thing that could be a problem!"

"It is if Bet doesn't love me."

"Do you have some reason to think she doesn't?"

Oh, yes, he had a reason. He would never forget finding Bet sitting before the glass wall and staring out into the moonstruck night. He would never forget that soft, plaintive whisper: *"John, John, why did you leave me?"* He had a reason, and it struck to his very soul, shredding any confidence he might muster. When Bet looked up to see him coming and a glad smile spread across her small face, he wondered whether she was wishing that he was her John. When she responded to his lovemaking, he wondered—until he felt as if the ghost of John Valentine was a rainy cloud following him everywhere he went.

"Jake?"

He raked his hands through his hair and sat back with a sigh. "She hasn't told me."

"Have you told her?"

"No."

His mother's head turned toward his father, her eyes bright and mocking. "This is the same boy who took all of those -ology courses and came home on his semester breaks talking to *us* about the 'communication gap'?"

"This is different," Jake defended himself.

"Oh? How?"

"Mom, you know why we married! Bet is happy with things the way they are. I can't..."

"Why not?"

"Because Bet has had so little in her life. I won't make her uncomfortable with this. If I tell her that I love her, and she can't return that love, it would make things awkward."

"But she does!"

"What?" Jake snapped up, black eyes glittering with surprise.

"Jake, Bet loves you. It's in her voice when she talks about you. It's in her eyes when she looks at you."

"You can't know that!"

"Can you know that she doesn't?"

His mother's words haunted Jake as the days slipped by. He seesawed between hope and despair. He argued with and against himself until he was exhausted by the emotional furor. At last he decided he had little to lose and everything to gain. He would tell Bet that he loved her.

— 10 —

"I'M GOING TO miss you and Bonnie, dear," Aunt Hester sniffed. "I hate to see you go, but I know Jake has missed you this week. Just look how he called every night."

He had, and every night it was the same. He said, "Hello," and she said, "Hello." He said, "How are you?" and she said, "Fine." She said, "How are you?" and he said, "Fine." He said, "How is Bonnie?" and she said, "Fine." Then they had nowhere to go. She couldn't tell him how much she missed him because she was afraid she would say too much. After two nights the joy of hearing his voice wasn't worth the pain of those long awkward pauses.

"You'll remember what I said?" Aunt Hester nudged aside her unhappy thoughts.

"I know you mean well..."

"Of course, I do! I love you both and want you to be happy! I tell you Jake is head over heels in love with you! It sticks out like a sore thumb—to everyone except you, you stubborn girl."

"Aunt Hester, you're confusing liking with—"

"Humph!" Her puckish blue eyes flashed. "No man who *likes* a woman looks at her the way Jake looks at you!"

Bet chewed a smile from her mouth. "And what way is that?"

"Like the only thing he can think about is getting you to bed!"

"Aunt Hester!" Bet's jaw dropped with shock.

"I'm old, child, not dead. That was just the way my Harry used to look at me. Ah, Harry," she mused aloud, "what a man. He knew how to make a woman feel like a woman, and I suspect that Jake does, too."

The speculative look that lingered on Bet's face brought a burning blush. She fidgeted and looked away. "That doesn't always have to be accompanied by love."

"There are none so blind as those who will not see," Aunt Hester quoted with disgust, rolling her eyes to the heavens. "Go on, hop in the car. And when you get home, open your eyes!"

Open her eyes. Bet thought about it on the hour-long drive south out of Shreveport. She braked for lights and slowed when needed. She entered the country and passed through alternating pine forests and rolling farmlands. And all the while her mind worked feverishly over a single question: Was it possible that Jake had come to love her? She picked apart his every word and look, but always she returned to that moment when he threw the cobbler through the window.

She turned off of the blacktop highway with its shimmering heat waves and followed the twists and turns of the gravel road to the Calloway Huddle. She knew Aunt Hester was wrong, but it didn't dampen her anticipation. In just minutes she would be with Jake again.

Her breath did funny little things in her chest as she pulled into the drive and rolled to a stop under the carport. Her initial impulse—to jump from the car and run to find him—faded. Her heart might pound painfully against her throat, but she mustn't allow Aunt Hester's forlorn hopes to push her into revealing how she felt. It wouldn't be fair to Jake, especially now with the baby coming. He might feel compelled to a pretense of love he didn't feel. She couldn't bear that. At least what they had now was honest.

The back door swung open, and Jake came out. Bet drank in the sight of him like a woman starved. His lean legs moved with potent masculine grace within the tight sheathing of faded jeans. The long sleeves of his blue work shirt were rolled up to form snug tubes around his biceps. He was smiling as he came around to her door, but by the time he leaned down to look at her, the smile was a dwindling memory beneath a haunting black stare that seemed intent on plundering her every thought. Could he? She looked down and then away and found her tongue tied by a crippling shyness.

It was ridiculous, she chided herself. This was Jake. Her husband. A man of laughter and compassion and warmth, but no Svengali to read her mind. She would betray as much with her awkwardness as she would by a blatant confession.

Hitching up her flagging courage like a man with a sagging pair of pants, she looked up at him once more. The last hint of the smile was gone. His formerly bright eyes held a dull, shuttered expression.

"Welcome home, Bet," Jake said quietly, extending his hand to help her out of the car. It was all he could do to hold his hand steady. He wanted to pull her out and crush her to him. He wanted to breathe deeply of her scent and bury his lips at her throat. He wanted to tell her of the niche she had carved in his heart and made uniquely her own. He might have found the confidence to do it if his resolution hadn't melted away with that unmistakable flare of fear he saw.

The fear was there, a quivering mass in the pit of Bet's stomach; the terror that she would betray herself and allow him to see the love that threatened to brim over in a complete loss of pride. She knew the humiliation

of giving love where it wasn't wanted. Her mother. Did
everything have to revolve around that dismal fact? And
there were others. The foster family after the Hunts. The
family that had no time or patience or love to give to a
lost and lonely little girl. Yes, she knew what it was,
and she had sworn—never again.

She tried to smile but couldn't force her lips to comply
with the frantic messages from her brain. Jake's hand
was warm and strong, and she clutched at it a little harder
than was necessary as she slid from the seat and stood.

"I missed...everyone," she finished lamely. The
simple act of saying, "I missed *you*" was too intimate
to fling over the barrier she felt rising between them.

The barrier was there, a palpable presence that Jake
experienced with a sinking heart. His mother was wrong.
His hand lingered around Bet's before it fell away. Sadness came like a fog creeping eerily across a marsh. He
wanted to shake her. He wanted to hold her. He wanted
to love her. What he did, instead, was press a chaste
kiss to her cheek. Was it his imagination? Did she lean
into him as though yearning for more? He tried to capture
her skittish gaze. When he couldn't, he moved to open
the back car door.

Bonnie slept soundly, slumping against the belts of
her car seat with her tiny lips pouted and drooling. Gently
Jake released her and scooped her, undisturbed, into the
cradle of his arms. Backing out of the car, he stood and
stared down at her round pink face. Here there was no
ambivalence, no hesitation. He didn't have to watch what
he said and did. He was free to love to his heart's content.

"I missed you, Puddin'head," he whispered tenderly,
unaware of how those words pierced the woman at his
side.

Bet swallowed the lump rising in her throat and toyed
with the car keys. Was it possible to be jealous of her
own daughter? She mentally shook herself. It was useless
to wish that Jake would look at her with his heart in his
eyes. Why did Aunt Hester have to plant that tiny seed
of hope?

"If you'll put her to bed," she said, hurrying around him to the trunk, "I'll get the suitcases."

"I can get them later."

"No," Bet responded, more sharply than she intended. "Please, just put Bonnie to bed. If we wake her, she'll be cross all morning."

She could feel him watching her as she fumbled the key into the lock. Then he was gone. She wrestled one suitcase out, and the other. Air whooshed, and the trunk closed with a snap. She would not cry. She would not hope. She would go on with her life as though nothing had changed. She would be beloved mother and unloved wife. Damn! She was feeling sorry for herself. What had that ever accomplished? It couldn't right a wrong. It couldn't change a fact. And the fact was she was married to a man who had never promised to love. She would not cry. She would not hope. And she would stop going around in circles!

That decided, Bet marched into the house with her chin set at a determined angle. She unpacked rapidly, hanging her clothes and putting her underwear away in drawers. She moved smoothly and efficiently—until Jake came to stand in the door. Suddenly she was all thumbs. Her makeup bag slipped from her hands with a clatter that scratched along her nerves, leaving raw, exposed wounds. A nervous glance flicked his way as she stooped to lift it. Why did he just stand there? Why didn't he say something?

He couldn't. Light conversation stuck in his throat, jammed tight against the desire to tell Bet that she had become the beating heart of this house and his life. He straightened when she hurried into the bathroom. It was absurd. He could let her out of his sight for a minute. She wouldn't vanish into thin air, he assured himself as he walked toward the bathroom door. He saw her stuff the bag into a drawer, then straighten to press her hands into her lower back as though it pained her. Their eyes met and locked in the mirror.

"Are you all right?" he asked.

"It's nothing." Bet's hands dropped to her sides, and she slipped past him. She felt as tautly strung as barbed wire and just as prickly. The fathomless black wells of Jake's eyes revealed not a glimmer of his thoughts. It irked her, that ability to hide within himself when she felt defenseless and vulnerable.

The downward tug of her lips was not lost on Jake. He frowned and felt a need to say something, anything that would thin the atmosphere, which was growing thicker by the moment.

"How was Aunt Hester?" It wasn't the most brilliant conversational ploy he had ever tried, but it was the best he could do for now. Dammit! What was wrong with Bet?

"Fine," she bit out as she snapped the suitcase shut. Aunt Hester was fine. Bonnie was fine. Jake was fine. Everybody was fine. Everybody except her! Why wouldn't he go away so she could have that cry she swore she wouldn't have?

Well, that got him nowhere fast, Jake thought with an edge of irritation. "You saw the Valentines?" Why was he asking these stupid questions when all he wanted to do was hold her?

"Yes," Bet answered tersely. The tears were boiling up inside her, a hateful, hurtful pressure.

"And?"

"And Nancy Valentine was her usual charming self. She's taking that poor man to court next week. That was all she could talk about. That and my refusal to join her in hounding him." The pressure was unbearable. It drew across her chest in a vise of pain and tore at her throat. If only Jake would go away and leave her alone. Just long enough to...

"So, why did you go to see her?" A spark of rage ignited in Jake. If that woman had hurt Bet...

"I didn't. I took Bonnie to see her grandfather. He, at least, loves her. Oh, damn!" Bet wailed and whirled away, swiping at the tears that spurted across her cheeks.

A sob caught her unawares, welling up and spilling out in a long, harsh groan.

"Bet?" Jake pulled her to him and held her tightly. For a moment it didn't matter how she had come to be there. All that mattered was that he could hold her as he had longed to do from the minute she arrived. But her sobbing soon lacerated that small pleasure. "Bet, that woman isn't worth a single tear. To hell with her and what she's doing! You can't change it. You can't change her."

Bet's head rose slowly, revealing tear-streaked cheeks and owlish eyes swimming with bewilderment. "What are you talking about?" she gasped out.

"Nancy Valentine! Isn't—isn't that why you're crying?"

How was it possible for one man to be so dense? "No, you—you big dumb clod!" Bet pulled away from him and scraped her knuckles across her cheeks. "I'm crying because I want to!" Her soft voice sharpened. "And you may as well get used to it, because all I do is sleep and cry when I'm pregnant!" Her horrified indrawn breath whipped into reverse and came rushing out in a long, keening lament. Then she was running for the bathroom and slamming the door behind her.

The sound vibrated through Jake, setting every nerve to twanging. Pregnant! Bet was pregnant! A fierce, exultant joy took flight but was soon shadowed by a cloud. Did Bet want the baby? It caught him square in the gut like the kick of a mule. She was tense and strained and unhappy. Because of the baby? Because of *his* baby? Was she wishing...

He could not finish that thought. Jake left the house with the slow steps of a man deep in unhappy thoughts.

The summer evening turned to a sapphire night spangled with stars. Bonnie slept in her crib. Bet lay in her bed, bathed, perfumed, and waiting.

She heard the distant sound of the door opening and

closing, then nothing. Raising herself up, she flicked on the bedside lamp and blinked her eyes against the flood of bright light. When she lay back, she saw Jake standing in the doorway with his boots in his hand.

"You're awake," he said dully.

"Are you hungry?"

"Just dirty."

His shower took longer than usual. So long, in fact, Bet began wondering if he were hoping she would be asleep when he came out. Just in case, she turned off the light and settled back into the pillow. The bathroom door opened, spilling light into the dark room. She caught a glimpse of Jake in his terry-cloth robe, his damp hair slicked back, before he switched the light off.

She sensed his movements through the darkness and heard the hushed whisper when he shed his robe. The bed sank, and he stretched out, lying perfectly still inches away from her. She listened to his breathing until she couldn't stand it anymore.

"Jake?"

"Yes?"

"I'm sorry."

"For what?"

"The way I told you about the baby. I—I didn't mean to do it like that."

"Don't worry about it. Mom says women in your . . . condition . . . get moody."

"You told them."

"Yes. They're happy for us."

"Are you . . . happy?"

"Yes," he said, but she heard him sigh and wondered what it could mean. "And you, Bet? Are you pleased?"

"Yes! Oh, yes! Very much." And she was. This didn't tear her in two with conflicting emotions and useless hopes. She wanted this child, Jake's child, to lavish with all the love she couldn't give to him.

He rolled onto his side and raised himself up on an elbow. "Are you sure?"

"I've never been more sure of anything."

"Slugger?"

His voice was like velvet coming out of the dark night to caress her. She watched his shadow loom nearer, and his lips found hers with unerring precision. They moved upon her mouth with a gentle persuasion that melted her bones with sensual lethargy. She felt the slight trembling in his hand as it moved from her waist and coasted to her breast. She wanted this. Every fiber screamed for it, but she found herself disengaging her lips and fending off his hand.

"Jake," she whispered breathlessly, "Jake, you don't have to do this now."

The muscles of his forearm bunched beneath her hand. "What do you mean?"

His voice scratched through the darkness like an old record, and Bet shivered. "We married for children, and now I'm . . . I'm pregnant. You don't have to . . ." Her voice trailed away.

If Aunt Hester was right, he'd tell me now. Tell me if you do, Jake. Please, tell me.

Mom was wrong. If she loved me, she wouldn't have done this. Damn!

"Good night, Bet," he said, and he rolled over.

Somehow that first sleepless night passed. Dawn released them from the agony of lying perfectly still in feigned sleep, but it brought a new set of problems: how to hide their disappointment and face each other. It wasn't as hard as either expected, since each was so determined to avoid the other. And so it went through that day and the next and a week of days—until Bet made a decision.

She ignored the persistent nagging ache in her lower back and galloped Rhapsody across the grassy field. The small herd of grazing Herefords raised startled white faces, bellowed, and scattered with flying tails. A tingle of excitement toyed with the pit of Bet's stomach. If she was being foolish, so be it. She wanted to see Jake, and she would. The excuse of bringing his lunch was perfect.

They had done little more than share meals since she got back, and she missed him. She wanted to see him smile his slow lazy smile. She wanted to hear the sound of his voice. She wanted to soak his presence into every starving pore. She was tired of being unhappy and uncomfortable. She might not be able to change how Jake felt, but she could change the way she acted. There was happiness in just being a part of his life. She wouldn't ruin that anymore with wishful thinking and the petulance of a thwarted child. She would find joy wherever she could and be glad for it.

Angling toward the gate, she brought Rhapsody to a halt and leaned down to lift the chain. Closing it behind her, she nudged her frisky mare into an exhilarating run that carried them toward a stand of oaks. Winding through the cool shadows at a walk, she came out onto another field and saw Jake on the far side.

He was taking up an old barbed wire fence. The hot sun beat down mercilessly on his bare back, which gleamed with rivulets of sweat. Bet watched, spellbound by the rippling interplay of muscles as he rocked the post back and forth. He stopped and pulled a gaudy handkerchief from his back pocket, swabbed it across his forehead, and stuffed it back in, leaving one bright corner standing up like a triangular flag.

Rhapsody sidestepped restlessly, and Bet patted her neck. "Come on, girl. Let's go feed that gorgeous man. That was *one* thing Aunt Hester was right about."

They trotted across the field, Bet smiling as Jake yanked the post from the hole with a heave that bulged a whole new set of muscles.

"That looks like the hard way to do it," she called out as she dismounted and tethered Rhapsody in the shade of a nearby sycamore. After smoothing her hand across the rump of Jake's gray stallion, she left the shade and walked toward her husband.

"It is." Jake gave her an uneasy glance as he laid the post aside.

"Don't you have—" Every thought fled when Jake stood. A huge droplet of sweat twinkled through the curling thatch covering his chest. Bet was mesmerized by its inching progress. It slipped and caught on a shaft of black hair that reflected the sunlight with a bluish sheen. Trembling and clinging as though terrified of letting go, it stretched thin, lost its tenuous hold, and streaked rapidly across Jake's burnished gold flesh. Snatching at another springy shaft, it hung on for dear life. Exactly what she would like to do.

She dragged her eyes away and wandered to the post hole. Nothing could have interested her less at that moment, but she studied it in spurious fascination. "Don't you have equipment to do this?" she asked, simultaneously wondering how her stiff, dry lips managed to wrap themselves around the words.

"Yes."

Short and to the point, like all their conversations these days. She sighed and raised an inquiring gaze. "Then why don't you use it?"

The whiff of a sardonic smile shaded Jake's mouth, but he didn't answer. Instead, his black eyes roamed across the gold-checked western shirt tucked neatly into her jeans, then drifted along the curve of her hips down to the boots he had given her for her birthday. Suddenly he froze.

"Bet, don't move! For God's sake, don't move!"

"Jake, what . . ."

She took a step forward, and he exploded. The back of his forearm caught her across the midriff, picked her up, and sent her flying. She hit the ground with a thump that knocked the breath from her, and she watched through a haze of tears as he jerked up the post and began pounding at the ground.

"Jake! Jake!" she cried. His head whipped around, and Bet flinched from the wild fury in his eyes. He pitched the post aside and flew to her.

"Jake, what . . ." He yanked her leg up, dumping her backward, and began tugging at her boot.

"Dammit, Bet, I told you not to move! God! Oh, God!" he breathed from the heaving bellows of his chest. Her sock went flying, and he began kneading her foot, examining every inch of it.

"What . . ."

"A ground rattler! Dammit, I should have kept you away from that hole! They nest in them!" And all the while he talked, his fingers raced over her foot, testing and caressing. "Thank God!" He slumped back onto his heels and cradled her foot against his chest with both hands. "He struck, but it didn't penetrate the boot."

"I'll . . ." Bet licked her powder-dry lips. "I'll have to tell Aunt Hester how useful your practical gift was." Her voice was shakier than she would have wished, and she shivered, feeling cold in spite of the heat. But the shiver that touched her then was nothing to the deep sensual shudder that racked her when Jake raised her foot and pressed it to his lips. His eyes stared over the tips of her toes, black, anguished, and glittering with . . . tears? Her throbbing heart pummeled the breath from her lungs.

His face was pale, almost sallow, beneath the healthy tan. He pressed her foot against his chest once more, and Bet's eyes dropped. She felt the convulsion of his hand across her arch and the pressure of his seeking eyes.

"Slugger, I . . ." he began, but stopped. Her gaze was drawn up to meet his, and she saw a turbulence that confused her. She heard him swallow and saw the nervous slide of his tongue across his lips. "I need you, Slugger," he said softly. "Is that enough for you?"

The question echoed through her mind like a challenge flung into a rocky gorge. Her eyes widened, and her breath closed around the scream that it was not enough. She wanted more, and the *more* she wanted froze her heart with dread.

"We agreed . . ."

"Damn the agreement!" Jake's face contorted with anger. "I'm talking about today and tomorrow and the rest of our lives!"

He released her foot and wrenched himself to his feet, taking a few jerky steps away. Standing with his back to her, he stared out toward the rim of the woods edged with a carpet of wildflowers whose color was dominated by the glaring yellow of bitterweed.

"I don't think I can go on like this," he said, almost as though he were talking to himself.

Bet's safe, secure world screeched to a sickening halt. She rose to her knees and jammed her clenched fists into the crevice between her thighs and huddled over as though she could ward off whatever he had to say.

"Bet, I know why we married, but . . ."

She heard the muted crackling of the dry grass as he walked toward her. His scuffed work boots entered her line of vision, then his knees as he knelt, almost touching hers, and finally his hands. They wrapped around her arms and pushed her up until she raised her face to him.

"Bet, people change. We can't stand still. Our feelings change, our needs change. When I married you, I thought I knew what I wanted. I thought I knew, but I was wrong. I—I . . ." His hands left her arms and cradled her face in his rough-textured palms. "God, Bet, can't you help me?"

She shuddered violently and felt the blood draining from her cheeks. "It—it isn't enough for you?" she asked, her voice high and tight with the chill of rejection.

"No," he said sadly. "No, it will never be enough."

Her pain was a thing alive, coiling and strangling and aching. She wanted to knock aside his hands and run screaming before he could say the irrevocable words that would send her away. The tears washed across her cheeks with a touch like ice, and she shook her head. "I—I don't know what you want, Jake."

"You!" he said fiercely. "I want you! I'm tired of sharing you with John Valentine's ghost! I want all of you or nothing! So choose, dammit, choose!"

Bet's lashes fluttered over her eyes, and her hands came up to hold his wrists. "But—but Jake, you have me."

"Not the way I want you," he said grimly. "I need more than a housekeeper and a fertile womb. I want a wife, a woman who loves me."

"You're asking me for more than you're willing to give?" she asked softly, her eyes clinging to his.

"Woman," he whispered as he trailed his thumb across her parted lips, "are you trying to drive me crazy? Can't you see?"

He fell silent, and a tiny shoot of hope took root in Bet's racing heart. "See what, Jake?"

A smile crept around the edges of his mouth and spread wide. "You won't make this easy for me, will you?"

"No," she breathed, her fingers digging into the bones of his wrist.

His cupped hands tilted her face up, and he leaned down to cherish her trembling lips in a timeless kiss. "My stubborn, maddening, beautiful Slugger," he said raggedly. "I love you. Do you . . ."

"Yes! Oh, yes!" And she laughed, a bright, happy sound ruffled in sunlight. She flung her arms around Jake's neck and was caught in a bone-crushing embrace. "I love you, Jake Calloway," she murmured fervently. "I feel as though I've loved you forever."

Their lips fused as he lowered her gently to the ground. Overhead the pale sky was brocaded with fleece. The pungent scents of wild flowers traveled on the sluggish breeze. Birds warbled a symphony, and bees droned in the background as they searched the cupped hearts of flowers for a nectar that was not half so sweet as that sipped by Bet and Jake.

Bet thought her heart would burst with pure joy. She was loved by this strong, sensitive man. She was free. His lips left hers to trail across her cheek and nuzzle the tender spot beneath her ear. Happy laughter bubbled within her and spilled out in a silvery peal.

Jake drew back and smiled his slow, lazy smile. "This is serious business, woman," he told her with a mock frown.

"The most serious," she agreed as she traced the upward tilt of his mouth and slanted a wicked look from beneath her lashes. "I promised myself once that I would be the tigress and you would be my prey."

One black eyebrow climbed, and his long, lush lashes flared. "Did you?" he growled.

"Uh-huh, and I think..." She pressed her mouth to his in a kiss that blossomed for her questing tongue. She tasted the corners of his mouth and skimmed across his lower lip and drew back. "I think this is the time."

His black eyes burned into hers. "Putty," he said in a resonant basso that was a vibrant reminder of the day she learned both the power and the flaw of shared passion. She would be the tigress, until her prey tired; then...

It was the quintessential battle. Neither could lose. She smiled, a small feline smile, and attacked with pliant lips that sought the pounding pulse at his throat and tasted the clean salt-sweat of healthy, hardworking man.

Bathed in sunlight and the heady gift of love, Bet played the tawny tigress to Jake's sleek black panther. He might moan and writhe beneath her tentative explorations, but his hot, slitted eyes watched her with an expression that promised his turn would come soon—very soon.

And it did. Jake purred deep in his throat, a sound that held agony and ecstasy. His fingers buried themselves in her hair, and he tugged her mouth to his and rolled atop her. The battle was lost... and won... and rejoined. As one they strove for the heights and captured the ephemeral colored ribbons of rapture.

"I love you, Slugger," Jake whispered.

Bet opened her eyes. She felt boneless, a puddle oozing satisfaction. "I love you."

He slid along her side and moved his hand reverently across her abdomen. "It's best this way, isn't it? For the baby?"

"Yes, it's best," she murmured softly, wondering why the gentle caress of his voice had darted through the inner regions of her heart and shattered her contentment.

— *11* —

SHE WAS WRONG. She had to be. Jake wasn't capable of faking something he didn't feel. There was no reason; they had their agreement. Had Aunt Hester betrayed her confidence? Was that it? He felt sorry for her. He couldn't! When he looked at her there was such tenderness in his eyes. But was that tenderness for her, or was it for the child she carried? Why did he say it? *It's best this way.* Why would he say that?

Bet's rapidly moving fingers stilled. The tiny bootie she was crocheting dropped to her lap. A wisp of a sigh escaped as she fought to will away incipient tears. Pregnant women had fancies, she reminded herself. That's all it was.

"Aunt Bet, you want a bowl of ice cream? I can bring a pickle, too, if you want it," Archie offered.

"A pickle?"

Jake plucked Bonnie off his stomach and rolled to his side to look up at Bet from the floor. "Pete told him that ladies who are expecting babies don't eat anything but pickles and ice cream." He grinned.

Bet laughed and crooked a finger at Archie. When he was close enough, she began to whisper in his ear. He drew back with an astonished expression.

"Crackers! You want crackers and ice cream? Yuk!" He swiveled about on a pair of tennis shoes that had seen better days and ran for the kitchen. "Mama, Aunt Bet wants crackers and ice cream! Yuk!"

The old farmhouse rocked with laughter as the men dragged their glazed eyes from the exhibition football game on television to present Bet with four matching expressions that echoed Archie's attitude.

"Try it; you'll like it." She laughed, though a faint tinge of color bloomed high on her cheeks.

"No, thanks!" four masculine voices gusted.

While his father and brothers turned their attention back to the game, Jake rubbed his hand up and down Bet's calf. "How are you feeling?"

"Hungry for salt and sweets. You know how these cravings are," she said lightly, sidestepping the question.

He frowned and cupped her ankle in a firm grip. "That isn't what I meant. How's your back?"

"Better." It wasn't, but there was no point in worrying him about it. She could worry enough for two. "You'll miss the home run if you don't watch."

"Woman, this is football! They don't have home runs! They have touchdowns!"

"Home run. Touchdown. Whatever." Bet shrugged with a tiny dismissing smile, but her tawny eyes glinted with mischief.

Jake pulled himself up and sat Indian-fashion with his back braced against the couch and his arm touching Bet's leg. "I can see I'll have to give you some lessons."

"Puh-lease, don't!" she laughed. Then she saw Archie returning. "Saved by the ice cream and crackers!"

Pete shouted and jumped from his chair. Even the quiet Burt was pulled to the edge of his seat, his massive fists bunched as he called, "Way to go!" Bet looked in time to see a runner drag two opponents into the end zone to score.

Bedlam reigned while Archie carefully handed her the bowl. He then pulled the remains of five crackers from his shirt pocket. It was more than likely, Bet thought with a twinge of dismay, that they had shared that temporary home with a small green frog or a chameleon or any number of squiggly creatures he was addicted to collecting. Unfortunately, he leaned against her knee watching curiously, so there was nothing to do but take a bite of ice cream and munch on a cracker.

"How is it?" Archie asked doubtfully.

"Good. Want a bite?"

"Nooo," he protested, his black eyes moving in a darting triangle from the bowl to the cracker to her face. Then he was off, skipping into the kitchen. "Mama, Aunt Bet's eatin' that stuff. Yuk!"

Jake chuckled and raised his hand with the palm flat. "Did anything peep at you?"

"No." She giggled and dumped the crackers into his hand. "But I'm sure something was in there."

"You can count on it. Did I ever tell you about the time—"

Whatever he was going to say was forgotten when pandemonium erupted in the living room and on the screen as the receiving team ran back for a touchdown. Bet watched the profile of Jake's quick smile as he discussed that mystery—the finer points of football—with his brothers. He did love her, she assured herself. He was thoughtful and considerate and seemed to sense her thoughts as soon as they appeared. Would he do that if he didn't?

She found she had lost her taste for ice cream and set the bowl aside. She was perverse. That was all there was to it. No sooner did she get what she wanted than she started questioning it. Her back twinged painfully, and she reached to rub the ache at her waist. It wasn't natural. There had been an occasional backache with Bonnie, but nothing like this. She was afraid, so afraid that something was wrong, and her recent call to her obstetrician had done nothing to alleviate that feeling.

Jake studied her with a clouded gaze. "Let's go home. You can rest."

"Why don't you stay and watch the game?"

"Uh-uh." He grinned. "I'd rather go home and snuggle with you."

It was late afternoon when Bet woke from her nap and discovered she was spotting. Terror lanced through her. It was too early for those fluttering signs of life that made a baby so real to its mother, but that didn't matter. This baby had been real to her from the moment she suspected its existence—a tiny new life to be nurtured and loved. She wanted to run but forced herself to walk.

Jake was puttering around the kitchen, concocting his special barbecue sauce for the steaks he planned to grill. "Evenin', sleepyhead. I—" The spoon slipped from his hand, clattering noisily on the counter. "What's wrong?"

"The baby," she said, her voice strained and shrill. "I'm going to lose the baby!"

"The baby?" The word sawed out of him in a guttural grunt that tilted upward into a question, as though it were something bizarre and unknown. "The baby! My God!" he groaned as he whipped off the canvas apron with its huge black lettering, WORLD'S GREATEST COOK, and rushed around the counter to sweep Bet into his arms. He bolted for the back door.

"What are you doing?" Bet asked.

"Taking you to the hospital!"

"You can't do that!"

"Why the hell not?" He stopped and glared down at her.

"There's Bonnie, and I should call the doctor first to see what he says."

"But you said—"

"I know, but I'm not sure! I should talk to Dr. Gregory!"

Jake carried her to the couch and laid her down as if she were a piece of crystal that could easily shatter. One dark hand trembled against her knee while the other wiped at the sweat that had begun dripping down his temples. "How do you feel, Bet? Are you in pain?"

"No, just my back. It—it's been getting worse."

"You didn't tell me?" he asked, his brow furrowed with anger and hurt.

She touched the fist knotted at his side. "I didn't want to worry you."

"Don't you know—" He stared down at her with a look that seemed to wonder if they would ever really understand each other. "Oh, hell!" He gave her a brusque, furied, loving kiss and went to make the call.

"Doctor! My wife is..." Pause. Jake hung over the kitchen counter, rubbing his fist across his forehead. "Well, who the hell is this?" He jerked up and paused to listen. "I know it's Sunday! But this is an emergency! My wife is..." Pause. "Yes! Yes! My name? Uh...oh, Jake Calloway!" Pause. "The patient? Elizabeth Calloway." Pause. His fingers drummed restlessly on the Formica, then came to an abrupt halt with a dull thud. "The problem?" His black eyes streaked toward Bet.

"Miscarriage," she said quietly, and she began to cry silent, hopeless tears.

"Miscarriage!" Jake boomed into the phone. "For God's sake, deliver this message immediately!" The bell tinkled when he slammed the phone into the cradle. He braced the heels of his hands on the edge of the counter, and his bowed head caught a glancing ray of the evening sun. The second slipped into a minute while he sucked in deep, slow breaths that escaped with a shuddering sound. At last his chin climbed from his chest, and his broad shoulders squared.

He went to Bet. Pulling her across his lap, he cradled her head in his big hand. "Cry, Slugger," he whispered. "Cry for both of us."

And she did. Her sobs wrenched through her and shuddered through Jake. She cried until she was exhausted, then lay on the couch staring into space while he tried to walk a hole in the rug. Back and forth Jake paced until Bonnie woke and began to cry. He hurried down the hall, looking almost pathetically grateful for a problem he could solve.

The phone rang as he brought Bonnie into the living room. He thrust her into Bet's arms and pounced before it could ring a second time.

Pause. "Archie? I . . ." Pause. Jake's black eyes rolled toward Bet. "Yes, I . . ." Pause. He fidgeted with the cord. "Yes, I think it's funny, too." Pause. "No, you can't talk to Aunt Bet right now. Archie, we're expecting a call. I'll have to hang up. We'll talk later."

The phone clicked into the cradle, and he smiled. "He tried the ice cream and crackers."

"I know." Bet made a feeble attempt to return his smile. "Yuk!"

"You got it."

The shadows were gathering to make their final assault on the day when the call came. Bet took it, feeling a tiny easing of her fear as Dr. Gregory's deep professional voice soothed, comforted, and calmed.

"What did he say?" Jake burst out before she could hang up.

"There's nothing to do but wait and see what happens. He wants me to go to bed and stay there."

"Is that all?" he bellowed in disbelief. "No hospital? No visit to see him? Nothing?" Bet shook her head helplessly, and Jake gave a short, pungent opinion of the medical profession. "We won't stay here," Jake added rapidly. "We're more than an hour from the hospital, and I'm not taking that kind of chance with you or the baby. I'll call Aunt Hester and tell her we're coming."

Jake wanted to leave Bonnie with his mother, but Bet would have none of it. She needed her daughter with her.

For three days Aunt Hester plied her with sassafras tea and encouragement; Carrie came after work and made her laugh with her office gossip and her recitation of all ten words Jake's cousin Richard had said on their first date; and Jake grew more haggard and gentle by the hour. But Bet got no better. The pain grew steadily worse. By the fourth morning it had stretched like a set of claws anchored to her backbone to dig into her abdomen.

Jake burst through the emergency room doors on the run. His boots skidded across the tile floor, the squared-off toes thumping against the baseboard as he clutched at the long counter to right himself. "Calloway," he said breathlessly. "Dr. Gregory called you about my wife?"

The nurse wrote rapidly in a file. "The threatened abortion?" she asked crisply, never raising her head.

The words slithered through his ear and coiled inside his brain. What made them sound so much more ominous than miscarriage? "Yes!" he shouted.

"Helen"—she never looked up—"the threatened abortion is here."

The threatened abortion! Rage choked Jake. Intellectually he knew it was necessary for a nurse to distance herself from the suffering she witnessed during every working hour, but this was *his* wife and *his* baby she was talking about! It was his beautiful, sweet, sensitive Bet who was suffering! It was his baby who might be dying at this very moment!

"Sir?"

Jake heard a metallic rattle and looked around to find a nurse unfolding a wheelchair.

"She's in the car."

They hurried through the doors, and the August heat hit Jake like a solid blow. Bet was hunched over, her forearms crossed over the ever-so-slight roundness of her belly. She was pale, and tears streaked down her cheeks in a steady stream as Jake lifted her and set her in the wheelchair.

"Bet?" he said softly, his thumb brushing across her cheek as he wondered if he would ever see her large and round with this child they both wanted so much. He felt a strange stinging in his eyes and blinked it away. He was a man, and men didn't cry. They let their wives do that for them, even if it was damned unsatisfactory. "How do you feel now, Slugger?"

"The same. Oh, Jake, I'm so scared!"

Her chin trembled, and her tear-flooded eyes were starred by the bright sunlight filtering beneath the roof. Jake's heart lurched in his chest. He tried to think of something reassuring to say, but there was nothing. Fortunately she was whisked away by the brisk nurse.

"You'll have to move the car to the lot, sir. If you come in this entrance, take the hall to the right. That will take you to the lobby desk, where you can fill out the paperwork. I'll take your wife to her room, number four-oh-five."

He came within an inch of having one wreck and causing another as he whipped into the street, but he was deaf to the honking horns and blind to the driver who leaned out his window to shake his fist. Paperwork! Bureaucracy! The bane of the modern world. Hell! Some ghoul would probably ask him to rise up off a slab in the morgue to sign one last document before he could be laid to rest!

Paperwork! He answered questions until he thought he would jump out of his skin. Bet was somewhere in this sterile vacuum, waiting for him. What was happening to her? He watched the cool, efficient young woman work over the computer console entering information from birth to . . .

He scrubbed at his burning eyes with his knuckles, raked his hands through his hair, and gave a disgruntled sigh.

"Sign these, Mr. Calloway, and you'll be done here."

Bet was curled into a fetal position on the hospital bed. Jake clamped his hand around the door to help support his shaky knees. He had to be strong for her, but his insides quaked like jelly. *Dear God, I can stand anything. Anything. Just don't take Bet.* He summoned up courage and calm but wasn't surprised when he couldn't find them. She looked so fragile huddled beneath the sheet. More child than woman.

He moved into the room, rearranging his tortured expression to a semblance of a smile. "I need you to massage my hand after signing all those papers," he said lightly as he perched on the edge of the bed.

"Poor Jake," she murmured lovingly, and she brought his palm to her lips.

"How do you feel?"

She gave him a tiny smile laced with pain. "You ask that every five minutes."

"I wonder it every second."

"The same," she sighed. "Dr. Gregory made rounds before you came. He isn't sure what's wrong and said we'll have to wait and see."

"Wait and see! Is that all he knows how to say?"

"He delivered Bonnie, Jake. I trust him."

Jake paced and sweated and paced some more. He stood at the window staring down at the traffic, staring out over the small business district to the tree-shaded residential area, staring into the azure sky cushioned with clouds. He wasn't sure just when he noticed, but by noon he had a full-fledged case of cramps. And there was nothing wrong with him! But he couldn't stand up. He couldn't sit still. He felt like a fool! His hand wandered across his belly and pressed.

"Jake, is something wrong?"

"No." He flushed brick-red and turned to the window.

"There is," Bet insisted. "Tell me."

Before he could think of a suitable reply, the nurse bustled in. "I've brought ice for you, Mrs. Calloway. Doctor's orders. Nothing to eat or drink, but you can suck on this if you're thirsty."

"Thank you." Bet pulled herself up onto the pillow. "Nurse, my husband isn't feeling well."

"Bet!"

"Oh?" Kindly hazel eyes expressed professional interest.

"I'm fine," Jake ground out.

"You aren't! Now, tell her. Maybe she can help."

"Bet," Jake groaned, but her determined expression

told him she was not to be thwarted. He could feel the blood gathering at his neck. "It's just cramps," he mumbled, feeling the blood plunge across his cheeks and burn into his forehead.

"I see. Do you feel ill?" the nurse asked.

"No!"

"Do you think you have a fever?"

"No!" God, this was embarrassing!

"I see," she said in a perfectly level voice. "It's possible you're suffering from sympathy pains."

"Sympathy pains!" Bet burst out.

"Oh, yes. Many husbands do that. Some even suffer through a kind of false pregnancy. They feel bloated. They have to go to the bathroom quite often. They suffer cramps during their wife's labor." She looked to Jake. "If it's something more, Mr. Calloway, come to the nurse's station. We'll see what we can do for you."

When she was gone, Bet turned an awed gaze on Jake. His eyes skittered away from the initial contact, and he dug his hands deeper into his pockets.

"Jake, is that what's wrong?" she asked softly.

"How the hell would I know?" he grumbled, digging the toe of his boot at the tile floor.

The long wait through the afternoon was broken by phone calls from the Calloway Huddle, Aunt Hester, and Carrie. One after the other, flower arrangements began arriving to brighten the stark room: a philodendron from Carrie, a bouquet of daisies from Aunt Hester, a bouquet of pinks and bachelor buttons from the Calloways.

After Jake had given up, the dozen red roses he had ordered on his dash upstairs arrived. The card read simply: *I love you. Jake.* He watched Bet read it and saw her clutch it to her breast and bend her head over it.

"I love you," she whispered. "I don't want to fail you."

"You couldn't, Slugger. You could never fail me."

He wanted to go to her and wrap her in his arms and protect her from all pain and hurt. He wanted to explain to her exactly what she had come to mean to him, but his feet were rooted to the floor and his tongue cleaved to the roof of his mouth. He wanted to share his agony of fear with her, but he was a man, and men were strong.

Evening came with serrated clouds edged in lavenders and pinks that darkened to rich, ripe colors before blending with the night. It reminded Jake of another sunset, another hospital room, another woman. Then, as now, he had been helpless to do anything but watch, wait, and listen to the frantic race of his own heartbeat.

Bet was worse. She said nothing, but she moved restlessly, and he could see the pain in her dull gaze and taut features. Wait and see. Wait and see. There had to be something more to do. Dammit! They wouldn't even give her anything for the pain!

"Jake? Jake!" Bet called out weakly.

He was at her side in an instant. "I'm here." Bending over the bed, he touched her face. Soothing words dried to powder in his mouth as his fingers recoiled from the clammy chill of her skin. The rapid rush of her breath fluttered against his wrist while he fought to control his own terrified panting. He reached up and flicked on the light. "Bet! Bet, look at me!"

She burrowed into a tighter ball. "Jake, it hurts! It hurts!"

He drew her up and stared down at the bruised eyes framed in her waxen face. So pale! She was so pale! The blood plummeted from his head in a giddy rush, and he staggered against the bed. He was a man. He had to be strong. He couldn't cry, not if it killed him. But he could go rushing down the hall like a madman. He could boom, "Nurse! Nurse!" in a stentorian voice that echoed four floors down every open stairwell. He could snag the startled gray-haired nurse who had the build of a Raiders' linebacker and drag her along behind him as if she were thistledown. He could stand there with his chest heaving and his eyes wild while she tugged her uniform back into place and said, "We must be calm, Mr. Calloway." It was the closest he had ever come to hitting a woman.

"Step outside, Mr. Calloway."

Outside? It ricocheted through his mind, connecting with nothing that made any sense. Outside? What was *outside?*

She caught his arm and gave him a push toward the door. "I must examine your wife."

The door closed behind him, and Jake leaned against the wall, shivering. It couldn't have been more than five minutes before the door opened and the nurse came out, but it stretched like the hours of an empty day.

"How is she?"

"I'm going to call her doctor."

"How *is* she?"

"The doctor will talk to you when he comes."

An athletic stride carried her away, and Jake glared after her in an impotent rage. The rage was strengthening. It fortified him to push the door open and join Bet.

She groaned softly when he sat on the bed. The sound tore into Jake, slicing away at the flimsy curtain of control he had drawn over his terror. If anything, she was paler than she had been. He willed himself to a numb blankness. The door whooshed open, and rubber soles padded quietly toward the bed.

"Dr. Gregory is on his way," the nurse whispered as she palpated Bet's abdomen. Jake's eyes met hers briefly, and he saw an uneasiness that was totally alien to her crisp efficiency. "I'll be right back," she said, and she hurried away.

It couldn't get any worse. He couldn't be more afraid. The outer limits had been reached. Bet's hand crawled into his, and he held it with a firm grip that paid homage to her fragility. It was the tie to sanity that kept him from falling over the edge.

Someone cried. Someone laughed. Visitors clicked down the halls on pencil-thin heels. Metal struck metal. Unoiled wheels squeaked.

The door whooshed open again. Jake heard the sound

of metal striking wood, and he looked around. The nurse wheeled in an IV stand. "Just in case the doctor wants it."

He turned back to counting the tiles on the floor, one by one.

"Jake?"

He put his face close to Bet's and brushed a tangle of hair from her temple. "What is it, sweetheart?"

"I'm sorry . . . the baby . . ."

"Hush," he soothed. "Don't worry. Don't worry about anything."

Dr. Gregory breezed in with his tie askew and a burgundy-colored silk handkerchief straggling from the breast pocket of his sports coat. Jake climbed off the bed and eyed him warily as he caught Bet's wrist and asked how she was feeling. Somewhere he had gotten the idea that the doctor was older, but his visions of a gray-haired patrician type with forty years of experience crumbled in the face of a man who looked no older than he did. Jake's eyes narrowed intently as the doctor prodded Bet's abdomen and frowned.

"Any bleeding, nurse?"

"A little spotting."

"I want a thousand cc's of D5R/L! Type match her for four units of blood! Get me an anesthesiologist! Call OR and get an operating room! Stat! She's got a possible ruptured ectopic pregnancy!"

"My baby! Noooo! Jake, my bay-beeee!" Bet's despairing scream echoed off the walls in ever-diminishing sounds that whispered into silence.

Jake lunged for the bed and caught her against his chest, one hand buried deep in her hair. She struggled for a moment, then clutched at him convulsively and went limp. Her head lolled back on his hand. "Bet! Bet!"

"She's fainted." The deep professional voice was tinged with sympathy. "We have to get her to surgery, Mr. Calloway. She's bleeding into the abdomen. I'm sorry, but there's no way to save the baby."

"Anything you have to do! Whatever it takes!" Jake's hand whipped out and snapped around Dr. Gregory's wrist. "Just save Bet!"

She was thirsty. Her mouth had an acrid taste, and her tongue felt swollen. She felt strange. Empty. Something was missing. She could hear an odd sound. Blip-blip. Blip-blip. She was tired. And cold. So cold. Except for her wrist. It was wrapped in warmth. She sighed and struggled to lift her heavy lids.

"Dr. Gregory?"

"You're awake. Good. How do you feel?"

Bet's lips trembled into a smile. "Like I could punch the next person who asks me that."

"Do you remember what happened last night?"

The emptiness. It was real. She felt the start of tears. "I lost my baby."

"Yes. There was nothing we could do to save it. I'm sorry."

"What . . . what is an . . . an . . ."

"Ectopic pregnancy. The egg was fertilized in the fallopian tube and attached itself there rather than traveling down to the wall of the womb. As it grew it stretched the tube until it finally burst last night."

"What did you do? Am I . . ." Her eyes drifted closed. "Am I sterile?"

"No. We removed one fallopian tube, but you have another. It is possible that you'll have a harder time getting pregnant in the future, but when you do, you should have no trouble carrying a baby to term. An ectopic pregnancy is rare, so you shouldn't worry about it again."

Blip-blip, blip-blip, blip-blip. The sound roared in Bet's ears. She looked across the room and saw the monitor with her heartbeats chasing one another across the screen in jagged, broken patterns. She dragged her eyes from it and picked at the sheet covering her.

"Do you mean . . ." She paused to lick her dry lips and steel herself to ask the question. "Do you mean that

I might never conceive another child?"

"Anything is possible, but you had no trouble conceiving Bonnie or this baby. It's very probable that you'll have more children. However, I want you to wait a year before you try again. Now, we'll have you moved out of ICU and back to your room."

He was gone, and she was alone. Really alone. There was no baby cradled in the comfort of her womb. No tiny life to nurture. No baby to love and dream for and about. No baby. And there might never be one. The tears began slowly.

It was an hour before she was wheeled to the OB ward on a stretcher. A nurse sailed by carrying a tiny blue-wrapped bundle to some happy mother. With a deep, avid hunger Bet watched the miniature fist that waved beyond the folds. The emptiness wasn't just with her now; it *was* her.

Jake was waiting for her. When they were alone he came to the bed and stared down like a thirsty man trudging toward a desert oasis. She had promised herself she wouldn't cry anymore, but she felt the tears welling. "I'm so sorry," she whispered.

He cleared his throat and reached out to touch her arm but seemed to change his mind midway and thrust his hand into his pocket. "Don't worry about anything. There's always tomorrow."

She rolled her head on the pillow and stared out the window. "There might not be. The doctor said . . ." Her voice trembled out of control. "He said I might have a hard time conceiving again. It's possible . . ." Could she say it? They were just words. Vowels and consonants strung together. Vowels and consonants that might mean the end of her dreams and Jake's dreams and—their marriage?

She bit her lip until she tasted blood, then drew a deep breath. "It's possible that I might never have another baby."

She heard the sharp intake of his breath but didn't

turn her head. She couldn't bear to look at him.

"Bet, I'm sorry. I know how much you want more children."

"So do you."

"Yes, but—but . . ."

She waited for him to go on, wondering what he would say. When he didn't, she rolled her head toward him. He'd moved away and stood now with his back to her. Tension arched along his nape. His shoulders shook once, and he drew a deep breath. They shook again, and Bet struggled up onto her elbow.

"Jake?"

"I—I have to go out for a while, Bet," he said, sounding strangled.

He strode toward the door, but when he got there he stopped. He reached for the knob, touched it, and his hand pulled away, slowly curling into a fist.

"If you can't have another baby," he said so softly Bet had to strain to catch it, "we'll both be disappointed. But we have Bonnie, and we can adopt. We can even be foster parents."

Jake turned slowly and walked toward her. His eyes glittered with a hard light that startled Bet until the light splintered and spilled over the fringe of his lashes. He sat on the bed and gently pulled her to him, and Bet felt the damp kiss of his tears against her forehead.

"Bet, I can do without anything in this world except you. I love you. I wish there were stronger words to say. I wish I were a poet. But I'm not. I'm just a man who can no longer imagine a life without you in it. I'm sorry about the baby, but you're alive, and I was so afraid . . ."

His chest heaved on a sob that turned to rueful laughter. One shaken hand cradled her face as he gazed down into her eyes. "Do you know what I did while you went to Aunt Hester's that week?"

"No," she said, not quite daring to believe what she was hearing.

"I went home to my parents. I felt like a prized jackass, running home to mother when I'm thirty-four years old, but I did it. I couldn't stand that house without you. The heart was gone from it, Slugger. The heart was gone from me. I've never experienced that kind of loneliness before, not even after—after Tricia's death. Do you know what I'm trying to say to you?"

Her smile was a quivering travesty, but the joy that could not blaze forth there shone in her eyes. Bet had come home. Home was not a house. It was not even a family. It was her niche in Jake Calloway's heart.

HEARTS VICTORIOUS

— 12 —

THE COOL AUTUMN rain streaked down the glass wall in sheets bordered with the pale golden light flickering from the hearth fire. Jake hunkered down to prod the glowing oak log with the poker, and sparks hissed up the chimney with a leaping flame that burnished his features with the rich patina of antique bronze.

Bet watched him with a lilting smile. The years had been kind to him. There were threads of gray in his black hair and a few sprinkling across the broad chest that was as strongly muscled as ever. Ten years. It didn't seem possible. She could remember the way his wary black eyes followed the swaying path of the mop she brandished as though it were yesterday. Yet, in another way, it seemed as though she had known him forever. It seemed that he had been a part of her as she was of him from the very beginning of her life.

Jake's slow, lazy smile slanted over his shoulder, waking her from her musings. "What'cha thinking, Slugger?"

"I'm thinking it's time for bed."

"To sleep?" he asked with a deliciously naughty quirk.

"Uh-uh."

He heaved a dolorous sigh. "What I have to put up with. I'm not getting any younger, you know," he complained with a wicked sparkle. "You wouldn't want to wear out—"

A lemon-colored pillow bounced off his back, and he came up with a playful if muted roar. Bet was scooped into his arms and treated to a kiss that metamorphosed from teasing to ravishing. At its end she snuggled her nose beneath his chin and sighed. "Lead on, Macduff."

"Rounds?" Jake groaned.

"Rounds."

His voice dropped in a deep, insinuating growl. "I had *other* things in mind."

"Patience is good for the soul," she responded primly, though she had to chew mercilessly on her lip to manage it.

"It wasn't my soul I was thinking about."

"It's good for that, too."

"Oh?"

There was a threat in the word. Knowing the minimal limits of her own patience when it came to *that,* Bet rolled out of his arms and held him off with a stiff finger. "Remember! You have to set an example!" With that, she whirled away and scampered into the hall, Jake hot on her heels. She paused to peek into Bonnie's room with a "Ssh!" for him that was unnecessary.

"Daddy?" Their daughter's delicate treble squeaked.

"Yeah, Puddin'head. You're not asleep?"

"Can I talk to you?"

Jake flipped on the light, revealing a dainty, befrilled room that suited Bonnie perfectly. She was a little lady, with her grandmother's drive to excel mellowed by her mother's gentle, sometimes mischievous, disposition. She loved her mother, but she worshipped Jake and idolized her cousin Archie, who was her current fount of all wisdom.

Jake ducked beneath the lacy French provincial canopy and perched on the side of the bed. He toyed with a springy curl that had darkened to a rich auburn. "What did you want to talk about?"

"My friend said I can't have two daddies. She said I can have only one, and he's in heaven. Is that true?"

"No, it isn't. When I adopted you that made you my little girl, but even if it hadn't, I would have been your daddy, because I've loved you and taken care of you from the first time I saw you. You and your mother were the best things that ever happened to me."

"Honest?" Bonnie's deep blue eyes gazed up at him in adoring, serious query.

"Honest."

"I'm glad." She sighed and smiled, a sweet smile that wrinkled her freckled nose. "I love you, Daddy."

"I love you, too, Puddin'head. Ready to sleep now?"

Bet leaned over Jake's shoulder to caress her daughter's cheek. "Sweet dreams."

"G'night, Mama. I love you, too."

A square of light brightened the hall after Bet flicked off Bonnie's light. Jake put his arm around her waist, pulling her into the curve of his body as they strolled toward it. The soft murmur of voices grew louder. Aunt Hester's happy laugh trilled, and Bet smiled. Though she was more frail than she had once been, Aunt Hester's blue eyes were as puckish as ever, and she hadn't lost a smidgen of her pleasure in life. She was eagerly awaiting the day when she could start matchmaking with Archie and Bonnie. Jake had taken that news with something less than grace. In fact, Bet giggled to herself, he had responded like a hornet whose hive had been threatened.

Another voice piped up, high and light. Jennifer, the squalling baby girl who had put to rest Bet's fears that she might never have another child. She was eight now; a tall, scrawny tomboy with huge tawny eyes and fine, flyaway black hair.

"Aunt Hester, I hate the name Jennifer!" she grumbled. "I wish I'd been named something else! Anything!"

"Not anything, child!" Aunt Hester protested. "Do you know that your mama and daddy wanted to name you after me? How would you like to go through life with a name like Hester?"

"Ugh!"

"That's what I've thought all my life. I never could think of myself as a Hester."

"If you could choose, what name would you want?"

"Scarlett," Aunt Hester sighed. "Katy Scarlett."

A burble of laughter escaped Bet, and she buried her face in Jake's chest. His arms came around her, squeezing painfully, while his chest heaved with silent chuckles.

"Aunt Hester, tell me again how mama and daddy met."

"It was a match made in heaven! I knew it would be! The first thing your mama did when she met your daddy was attack him with a mop!"

"She didn't!" Jenny squealed, just as if she hadn't heard the tale a hundred times already.

"She did! He went . . ."

Her voice faded as Jake and Bet moved down the hall toward the sliver of light peeping from a suspiciously closed door. Grunts and shouts and thumps hurried their steps.

Jake threw open the door, and all action came to a screeching halt. The seven-year-old twins, Jason and Justin, whirled around, battered pillows clutched in their hands. Black eyes blinking and black hair tumbled in masses of curls across their foreheads, they stood frozen amid a drifting snow of goosedown that clung to snub noses and flat ears and glossy eyelashes. Suddenly they sprang apart, diving into their beds and squirreling under the covers.

"He started it!" echoed two muffled voices.

Bet chewed away a laugh and tried to look properly chastened when Jake gave her a frown that dared her to say a word.

"I will see you two in my study tomorrow morning, first thing," Jake thundered. "If we hear a peep out of you for the rest of the night..."

He let that hang, and the matched set of noses inched from beneath the covers. "We'll be good," they echoed, casting pleading gazes at Bet.

"Don't look to your mother! She won't get you out of this one. Tomorrow morning!"

"You won't be too hard on them?" Bet whispered as they returned to the hall, leaving a hushed silence behind them.

"Am I ever?" Jake grinned. "I think there ought to be lessons in sternness for mushy parents."

Baby Joel slept peacefully, his small diapered rump pointed at the ceiling. Bet and Jake lingered over the crib, discussing the excitement of his first tooth in whispers before moving into their room.

Rounds were over, and minutes later Bet and Jake were snuggled beneath the covers of their own bed.

Bet's fingers tiptoed across his collarbone. "Sleepy?"

"Uh-uh." Jake wafted the breath of a kiss across her temple and sighed, a sound of utter peace and blissful contentment. "It's a good life, isn't it, Slugger?"

"The best," she agreed. "The very best. And it'll get even better if you turn over," she purred.

"Am I about to get ravished?" he asked, his voice trembling with laughter.

"Uh-huh."

Jake wasted no time complying, and Bet trailed tempting fingers across his nape before pressing light butterfly kisses down the shallow valley of his spine...

WONDERFUL ROMANCE NEWS!

Do you know about the exciting SECOND CHANCE AT LOVE/TO HAVE AND TO HOLD newsletter? Are you on our *free* mailing list? If reading all about your favorite authors, getting sneak previews of their latest releases, and being filled in on all the latest happenings and events in the romance world sound good to you, then you'll love our SECOND CHANCE AT LOVE and TO HAVE AND TO HOLD Romance News.

If you'd like to be added to our mailing list, just fill out the coupon below and send it in…and we'll send you your *free* newsletter every three months — hot off the press.

☐ *Yes, I would like to receive your **free** SECOND CHANCE AT LOVE/TO HAVE AND TO HOLD newsletter.*

Name _____

Address _____

City _____ **State/Zip** _____

Please return this coupon to:

Berkley Publishing
200 Madison Avenue, New York, New York 10016
Att: Rebecca Kaufman

74

Second Chance at Love.

All of the above titles are $1.95
Prices may be slightly higher in Canada.